Welcome to the Secret World of Alex Mack!

How did I end up in this freezing lake at night, hiding from the Chemical Plant goons? I was only trying to help Ray out—he wanted to get a big scoop for the newspaper where he works delivering papers. I guess he thought it might get him a job as a reporter! But suddenly we're caught up in something that may be bigger than both of us can handle. We're going to need some real help . . . and fast, before my powers become front page news. Let me explain. . . .

I'm Alex Mack. I was just another average kid until my first day of junior high.

One minute I'm walking home from school—the next there's a *crash!* A truck from the Paradise Valley Chemical plant overturns in front of me, and I'm drenched in some weird chemical.

And since then—well, nothing's been the same. I can move objects with my mind, shoot electrical charges through my fingertips, and morph into a liquid shape . . . which is handy when I get in a tight spot!

My best friend, Ray, thinks it's cool—and my sister Annie thinks I'm a science project.

They're the only two people who know about my new powers. I can't let anyone else find out—not even my parents—because I know the chemical plant wants to find me and turn me into some experiment.

But you kno̲ ̲̲̲̲̲̲s I'm not so average anymo̲

The Secret World of Alex Mack™

Alex, You're Glowing!
Bet You Can't!
Bad News Babysitting!
Witch Hunt!
Mistaken Identity!
Cleanup Catastrophe!
Take a Hike!
Go for the Gold!
Poison in Paradise!

Available from MINSTREL Books

For orders other than by individual consumers, Pocket Books grants a discount on the purchase of **10 or more** copies of single titles for special markets or premium use. For further details, please write to the Vice-President of Special Markets, Pocket Books, 1633 Broadway, New York, NY 10019-6785, 8th Floor.

For information on how individual consumers can place orders, please write to Mail Order Department, Simon & Schuster Inc., 200 Old Tappan Road, Old Tappan, NJ 07675.

NICKELODEON®

the secret world of

ALEX MACK™

Poison in Paradise!

Diana G. Gallagher

A MINSTREL® BOOK

Published by POCKET BOOKS
New York   London   Toronto   Sydney   Tokyo   Singapore

The sale of this book without its cover is unauthorized. If you purchased this book without a cover, you should be aware that it was reported to the publisher as "unsold and destroyed." Neither the author nor the publisher has received payment for the sale of this "stripped book."

This book is a work of fiction. Names, characters, places and incidents are products of the author's imagination or are used fictitiously. Any resemblance to actual events or locales or persons, living or dead, is entirely coincidental.

A MINSTREL PAPERBACK *Original*

A Minstrel Book published by
POCKET BOOKS, a division of Simon & Schuster Inc.
1230 Avenue of the Americas, New York, NY 10020

Copyright © 1996 by Viacom International Inc., and RHI Entertainment, Inc. All rights reserved. Based on the Nickelodeon series entitled "The Secret World of Alex Mack."

All rights reserved, including the right to reproduce this book or portions thereof in any form whatsoever. For information address Pocket Books, 1230 Avenue of the Americas, New York, NY 10020

ISBN: 0-671-00083-7

First Minstrel Books printing October 1996

10 9 8 7 6 5 4 3 2 1

NICKELODEON and all related titles, logos and characters are trademarks of Viacom International, Inc.

A MINSTREL BOOK and colophon are registered trademarks of Simon & Schuster Inc.

Cover photography by Tom Queally

Printed in the U.S.A.

For my nephew, Brian Sands,
with love and gratitude
for his enthusiastic support

CHAPTER 1

"Thanks for helping me out today, Alex," Ray said as he shoved rolled newspapers into the big pockets of his carrier bag. Alex Mack and her best friend, Raymond Alvarado, were in the gigantic loading area of the *Paradise Valley Press*, stocking up on newspapers to deliver on Ray's route.

"No problemo," Alex said sincerely. "You've been waiting two weeks to see the sneak preview of *Star Pirates.* And there's no way you could have finished your route and gotten to the theater by six-thirty without my help. Besides, you're always there for me when I need you. I'll never be able to repay all the favors I owe you." Alex grunted as she lifted her own stuffed carrier. She slipped her head through the opening separating the front and back pouches, sagging as the weight settled onto her shoulders. Then she pulled her long blond hair out from under the canvas carrier and adjusted the bag so the weight was even.

"I'm not into keeping score, Alex, but this will make up for a few of those favors," Ray said. "And you know how important this movie is to me. There's not much point in going to a movie if you miss the first half-hour."

"There's also no point in going if you don't have time to get a bucket of popcorn and a root beer," Alex added. "What happened to Louis, anyway?" she asked curiously. She didn't mind helping Ray deliver newspapers, but Louis Driscoll had promised to split the route with Ray a week ago. He had backed out today at the last minute.

"Detention." Ray shook his head. "He thought it would be a kick to grease the climbing ropes in the gym. But the kid with the rope burns on his legs wasn't laughing. And Mr. Rooney didn't think it was so funny either."

"I can imagine." Alex giggled. "Mr. Rooney has an H.Q. only slightly above zero."

"H.Q.?" Ray looked puzzled.

"Short for humor quotient," Alex explained. "You know, like I.Q. is short for intelligence quotient."

"Oh, right! Gotcha." Ray laughed, then fixed Alex with a worried stare. "You've been hanging around your sister the brainiac too much."

"I sound like Annie?" Pretending to be horrified, Alex inhaled sharply and smacked the side of her face.

Ray laughed, then waved to someone behind her. "Hi, Mr. Hardwick!"

Alex glanced over her shoulder and saw a tall, thin man with a weathered face and silver hair across the room. Ray had told Alex all about Mr. Hardwick—how he was a great reporter and always up on the local news. Ray idolized the man and was hoping someday he could be just as good a journalist.

"He's got the coolest job," Ray said. "He's always the first one to know what's happening. Someday I'm going to be a real newshound with my own beat."

"Where'd you learn to talk like that? Now *you* sound like Annie," Alex said.

Ray just shrugged and then smiled at Mr. Hardwick as he walked over. "How's it going, Ray?"

the man said. "I thought I'd get out of the news-room for a moment to stretch my legs."

"Just fine," Ray said. "Alex, this is Mr. Hard-wick, senior editor of the *Paradise Valley Press.*"

"Hello, Alex." Mr. Hardwick smiled warmly and extended his hand. "Giving Ray some help today, are you?"

"Yes, I am." Alex shook the editor's hand. "That's okay, isn't it? I've helped him before and I know the route."

"That's fine. I don't care as long as the papers get delivered." Mr. Hardwick pulled a newspaper out of Alex's pack and unfolded it. "I just wish you were delivering a paper that was worth reading."

"Huh?" Ray looked confused.

"This isn't news, Ray! Just look at this head-line."

Mr. Hardwick slapped the paper, then turned the front page toward them. The headline read: AUTUMN FLOWER SHOW OVERBOOKED. Below it was a picture of several people protesting outside the Town Exhibition Hall.

"This is the big news of the day," Mr. Hard-wick grumbled. "Owing to a clerical error, some of the exhibitors have to set up in the hallways."

"Not very exciting, huh?" Ray said.

"No, Ray, it's not." Mr. Hardwick sighed as he put the paper back into Alex's pack. "There hasn't been a decent story in this town since that chemical plant truck accident two years ago."

Alex and Ray exchanged cautious glances.

Sticking her hands in her jeans pockets, Alex tried to look casual, but her stomach twisted a little.

"And even that story fizzled," Mr. Hardwick went on. "Danielle Atron, the chief executive officer of the plant, put pressure on the media to keep the incident out of the news. So nobody ever proved that a kid was contaminated with the chemical. The bit about the kid was just hearsay. A good newspaper person doesn't print rumors, Ray. We need cold, hard facts."

"And we *never* reveal a source," Ray added emphatically.

Alex blinked. *We?*

"Never." Shaking his head, the editor stared wistfully at the ceiling. "What I wouldn't give for a solid, newsworthy story that's fit to print."

"Like what, Mr. Hardwick?" Ray asked.

"Like the identity of that kid in the accident— if there was a kid. Why doesn't anyone know who it was?" The editor's face lit up with excitement as he talked. "Was the kid hurt? Did Danielle Atron bribe the parents so they wouldn't talk? And if she did, what's the plant's CEO trying to hide?"

Alex shifted uncomfortably. She didn't need a news-hungry editor digging into the details of the accident. A good reporter might find out what had really happened that day.

Ray scowled thoughtfully. "What would you give, Mr. Hardwick? For a major scoop, I mean."

Startled, Alex stared at Ray. She knew he wouldn't tell Mr. Hardwick the real story about the GC-161 accident. To prove that a kid was involved, Ray would have to produce the kid, and Ray wouldn't do that to her. He hadn't turned her in to Vince last year when he was mad at her and needed the reward money to buy concert tickets. But now it looked as if Ray was hatching some kind of scheme. She could almost see the wheels turning in his head.

Mr. Hardwick started to laugh at what Ray was suggesting. He stopped abruptly when he saw Ray's intent expression. "Interested in doing some investigative reporting, Mr. Alvarado?"

"Why not?" Ray said. "I'm out there on the

streets every day. I mean, on the beat. I see things, hear things. I might uncover something big— something that would set this town on its ear. I've got a nose for news."

"Is that so?" Mr. Hardwick hid a smile with his hand and nodded. It was obvious to Alex that the editor didn't take Ray seriously, but he didn't want to discourage him, either.

"Tell you what." The editor clamped his hand on Ray's shoulder. "You get a story like that, and I'll give you the byline and a bonus check."

"What's a byline?" Ray asked.

"It's a line printed at the top of the story, stating your name."

"Oh, wow!" Ray said. "And do I get a promotion from delivery boy to reporter?"

"Scoop first, Ray. Then we'll talk."

"I'm on it, Mr. Hardwick."

Alex waited until Mr. Hardwick was out of earshot before teasing Ray. She didn't want to embarrass him in front of the editor, but his career aspirations changed every couple of weeks and she couldn't resist.

"Okay, Scoop." Edging closer, Alex tugged her baseball cap down and nudged him. "Fill me in.

Got a hot tip? Some inside info you haven't told me about?"

"What's with you, Alex?"

"I wanna know what you're planning to do."

Ray didn't look at Alex as he said, "Deliver these papers as fast as possible, so we don't miss the start of the movie." He put on his carrier bag and adjusted the shoulder straps.

Alex hesitated as he hurried out the door for his bike. Why was Ray being so secretive? She had expected him to plunge into the role of reporter because he liked throwing himself into whatever profession had recently captured his interest. *But why isn't he playing it up like usual?* she wondered. *Unless he isn't playing!*

Slowed down by the bulk and weight of the newspapers, Alex telekinetically lifted the carrier off her shoulders so she could run out the door faster. But Ray was already on his bike when she caught up. *Oh, no. Not so fast, Ray,* Alex thought. And then she threw an electromagnetic force field around the bike to keep him from leaving.

"No fair, Alex. Let me go."

Removing the force field, Alex planted herself in front of Ray's bike. "What's going on, Ray?"

"Nothing." Ray started to pedal away.

Alex grabbed his handlebars. "You know something, don't you? You wouldn't have told Mr. Hardwick you could get a news scoop unless you thought you really could. So what do you know?"

"Nothing," Ray insisted stubbornly, looking at the ground. "It's just a hunch, and investigative reporters don't talk about their hunches, Alex. That's how they lose their exclusives."

"I'm not going to steal your story, Ray; you know that. I'm just worried that you'll get into something over your head. Besides, maybe I can help."

"You don't want to, Alex. Believe me." Ray looked off into the distance, his mouth set in a tight line.

"Why not?"

Ray hesitated, sighing deeply. Then he turned to Alex, finally looking her in the eye, and said, "Because I'm going to investigate Paradise Valley Chemical."

CHAPTER 2

"This is a really, really bad idea, Ray. On a scale from one to ten, I'd say that's about a zero."

Perched on the washing machine in the Mack garage, Alex watched Ray pace. After the movie yesterday, he had refused to discuss his decision to investigate the chemical plant because he said he didn't have a plan—yet. Alex had tossed and turned all night and fretted all morning. Annie had been so annoyed at all her fidgeting that she had gone to her friend Linda's house to work on an English essay. Then, finally, after lunch, Ray had returned one of her many calls and said he was coming over. At least it was Saturday and Alex didn't have to sit through hours of school, worrying and wondering about what he intended to do.

"No, it isn't, Alex. It's a brilliant idea." Eyes shining with enthusiasm, Ray stopped and faced her. "For one thing, we're the only ones who know that the plant is making illegal compounds. Except for Annie, and she isn't talking."

"And neither are we, Raymond! We can't say anything about GC-161. It's too big a risk. We could get into trouble with Danielle Atron. And besides, my dad is working on that project."

"But he doesn't know he's doing the kind of experimental research the government banned."

"We know that. The government doesn't." Sliding off the washer, Alex crossed her arms and set her jaw. She could be just as stubborn as Ray. "GC-161 is out, Ray. Period."

"I wasn't going to write a story about GC-161, Alex."

Alex threw up her hands. "Then why did you bring it up?"

"Listen," Ray said patiently. "If Paradise Valley Chemical is developing illegal compounds like GC-161, they might be doing something else illegal, too."

"Like what?"

Ray shrugged. "That's what I have to find out."

"There's nothing I can say to talk you out of this, is there?" Alex had to ask, even though she already knew the answer.

"Not a thing. I've made up my mind."

Alex sighed. If Ray had made up his mind to be an investigative reporter, he was going to be an investigative reporter, at least for the next few days. However, if she could steer him onto a subject other than Paradise Valley Chemical, he might start losing interest in being a member of the press before he got into serious trouble.

"Okay, Ray, but maybe you should start out with an article that isn't quite so—ambitious. Write another story first and work up to doing an exposé on the chemical plant."

"No way! Getting the goods on Paradise Valley Chemical is my chance to break into the news game at the top. I might even win the Pulitzer Prize for journalism with my very first story." Ray's eyes glazed over as he imagined his moment of glory.

"Ray?" Rolling her eyes, Alex raised her voice. "Ray!"

Snapping back to the present, Ray eyed Alex pointedly. "There's another angle to consider," he said. "If I can prove Danielle Atron is up to her neck in some other nasty business, maybe Mr. Hardwick will forget about the GC-161 accident."

"Think so?" Alex said.

"Yeah. He doesn't care what scoop he gets as long as it's dynamite news."

That idea appealed to Alex in a big way. Gigantic black newspaper headlines identifying her as the GC-161 kid had punctuated her dreams the night before. *No, they weren't dreams*, Alex thought. *They were more like nightmares.* Her life would be ruined if anyone found out what had happened to her. She had to get both Mr. Hardwick and Ray thinking about something else.

"Okay, Ray. I'm in." She had no idea what she had just gotten herself into, but she felt it was her only choice.

"No, Alex. It's too dangerous—"

The kitchen door flew open. "What's too dangerous?" Mr. Mack asked as he walked in.

"Uh—ice hockey," Ray said quickly. "I don't think I'll go out for the team this winter."

"A wise decision." Mr. Mack leaned against the doorjamb. "I never tried out for ice hockey myself, but one of my best friends in college made the team. He never actually played a game, though. Quit after he lost two teeth in practice."

"Really?" Ray nodded and shifted his weight. "What's new at the plant these days, Mr. Mack?"

"Not much. Just working long hours under a lot of pressure, as usual."

"What are you doing in here, Dad?" Alex asked, wanting to change the subject.

"Today I am going to clean the garage!" Mr. Mack announced with great conviction. Picking up a pile of newspapers stacked on the dryer, Mr. Mack hesitated, then stepped over to a row of trash cans.

"Now?" Alex felt the blood drain from her face. The clothes she had been wearing the day of the accident were in boxes on the shelf behind the trash cans. She and Annie had never figured out a safe way to get rid of them, since they were covered with dried GC-161. "You're going to clean the garage *now?*" Alex asked in a thin voice.

"It's a big job, Alex. If I don't start now, it won't get done this weekend." Setting the newspapers on top of the GC-161 storage boxes, Mr. Mack reached for the lid on a trash can marked Newspapers.

"That's for sure—" Ray's eyes widened as the

newspapers began to slide, dragging the unbalanced GC-161 storage boxes with them.

Alex muffled a gasp and "thought" the newspapers and boxes back onto the shelf before they fell and broke open. Using telekinesis under her dad's nose was risky, but not as risky as letting him find the evidence that linked her to the GC-161 accident.

Mr. Mack didn't notice. He was staring into the trash can with a look of disgust. It was full to the brim with old newspapers, waiting to be recycled.

"Does Annie know about this?" Alex tried not to sound as alarmed as she felt.

In addition to the gold-gunked clothes, all of Annie's research on GC-161 and Alex was stored out here. The Macks had been stashing junk in the garage for years, and it had seemed like a perfectly safe place. Every now and then her father mentioned cleaning it out, but he had never gotten around to it—until today.

"I gotta go." Waving, Ray backed toward the outside door. "Later, Alex."

Alex hesitated, torn between stopping her dad before he knocked over the boxes again and stopping Ray before he began his investigation without her.

"I've been asking Annie to straighten things up in here for weeks." Putting the lid back on the trash can, Mr. Mack picked the can up and headed out the side door. "She's had plenty of warning."

A lucky break, Alex thought as she dashed out behind her father and ran after Ray. She only had a couple of minutes, though. Desperate, she telekinetically tugged on Ray's jacket to slow him down. "Ray! Wait!"

Ray faltered as the back of his jacket stretched taut. "I really wish you'd stop doing that, Alex."

"Sorry, but this is important."

"More important than your dad poking around the garage?"

"He's taking out the trash, but I only have a minute." Alex spoke in a rush. "Look, Ray. I know that investigating the chemical plant is dangerous. That's why I wish you'd change your mind, but since you won't, you've got to let me help you. You can't do it alone."

Ray started to protest again, then gave in. "All right. Your powers might come in handy if we get into a tight spot."

"Right. Now you're talking," Alex said. "So where do we start?"

"I'm still working that out. I'll call you later. Promise."

Certain that Ray would keep his word, Alex raced back to the garage and almost collided with her father in the doorway.

"Whoa, there! What's the hurry?" Mr. Mack frowned in concern. "Everything okay between you and Ray?"

"Fine. He's just got a lot to do today." Alex followed her father inside. She hadn't had much luck stopping Ray from digging into the chemical plant's activities, but somehow she *had* to stop her father from cleaning the garage—at least until Annie could collect all the GC-161 stuff and hide it somewhere else. Alex didn't have a clue where Annie had stored it all.

"Where's Mom?" Alex watched anxiously as her dad checked the second trash can. It was full, too.

"She started her tennis lessons today." Sighing, Mr. Mack dragged the heavy can toward the door.

"Tennis? Since when is Mom interested in tennis?"

"Since she agreed to be Valerie Lincoln's partner in that benefit tournament at Lakewood next weekend. Mrs. Lincoln plays all the time, but your mom hasn't been on the courts in years. She doesn't want to make a complete fool of herself— especially playing doubles with the mayor's wife." Grunting, Mr. Mack lifted the can and staggered out the door.

Grabbing the stack of newspapers off the storage boxes, Alex took them to the curb. Her father groaned and rubbed his back as he set down the second trash can and straightened up.

"It's such a beautiful day," Alex said brightly. "There must be something else you'd rather be doing instead of cleaning the garage. Maybe you could play tennis with Mom after her lesson— help her get in some more practice."

"That's a good idea, Alex, but the garage is a priority. I've been putting it off for years, and it just can't wait any longer." Sighing again, Mr. Mack trudged back up the driveway.

Frantic, Alex jogged up beside him. "I'll do it, Dad. I'll clean the garage."

Surprised, Mr. Mack faltered. "Well, I appreciate the offer, but it's an awfully big job—"

"I can do it, Dad, really. Mom needs you to help her improve her game. This tournament is a big deal, right?"

"Right, but—"

"So I'll clean the garage. Nicole's visiting her grandparents, Robyn's babysitting, and Ray's busy, so it's not like I'll be missing out on anything today."

"Okay, but I expect the job to be done and done right," Mr. Mack said sternly.

"It will be," Alex said earnestly. "Promise."

"Well, all right, then. The job's yours." Mr. Mack looked at his watch. "Guess I'd better change and get to the courts."

Alex's eager smile faded the instant Mr. Mack disappeared through the front door. Going back into the garage, she paused in a small, bare spot in the middle of the floor and looked around in dismay. Tools and magazines, old clothes and broken toys, obsolete kitchen appliances, flower-pots, bottles, and rusty cans were piled to the ceiling on top of cardboard boxes whose contents had long been forgotten. Metal shelves and plastic milk crates overflowed with odds and ends of hardware. The workbench was covered with Annie's experiments, and the space under the train table was crammed with boxes of notebooks and scientific equipment.

So where to start? Picking up a soiled rag lying at her feet, Alex dropped it in the closest trash can, which was already overflowing. Then she just stood there.

Two hours later, Alex had not made any significant progress except for shifting a few boxes to different spots. Even using telekinesis, moving things took time and energy. And she didn't dare throw out anything that Annie could be using in an experiment. The cans and bottles could have some mysterious purpose—what *was* that foul-smelling green stuff in the former peanut butter jar, anyway?—and the old magazines and newspapers might contain important articles Annie wanted to save for research.

Alex had to sort through the crates and piles of junk by hand, and it was a hopeless task without her sister's help. Annie would have some idea about what should be kept and what could be tossed. Earlier, Alex had tried to reach Annie at Linda's house, but the answering machine had picked up. Plus, she couldn't stop worrying about Ray's determination to nail Paradise Valley Chemical. Alex was at a loss.

When the telephone rang, she grabbed the cordless phone off the drier and sat cross-legged on the floor. "Hello."

"Alex?"

"It's me. What's up, Ray?"

"Meet me in front of your house at ten to-night," Ray said in a clipped, no-nonsense mono-tone. "Wear black."

"Wait a minute. What—"

"Can't talk now. This isn't a secure line."

"But what are you planning to do tonight?" Alex asked.

It was too late. Ray had already hung up. It didn't really matter, though, Alex thought with a sigh. Because she knew all too well what Ray had planned for this evening.

Ray was going to spy on the plant.

And she had agreed to help him.

CHAPTER 3

Sneaking out of the house to meet Ray at ten o'clock was easier than Alex had hoped. Her parents were so exhausted after playing tennis all afternoon, they had gone to bed early. Annie was staying overnight at Linda's instead of coming home after a foreign film festival at the library. Alex hadn't talked to her yet, so Annie still didn't know about the garage problem. But that could wait until tomorrow.

Ray couldn't.

"Pssst. Alex!" Ray slipped out of the bushes by the Macks' house. With his black clothes, he was almost invisible in the moonless night. A black bag hung over his shoulder. "You look great," he said in a loud whisper.

"Great is hardly how I'd describe it," Alex muttered. Black was not one of her favorite colors, but she had managed to find clothes suitable for the job at hand. Her own black leggings were perfect, and she had borrowed her mom's black snow boots and gloves, Annie's black turtleneck, and her dad's ski mask.

"I really think you should reconsider this, Ray. What—exactly—are you planning to do?"

"We're going to watch the plant to see if anything weird is going on." Ray lifted the ski mask off her face. "Keep it up until we get there. Wearing it over your face on the sidewalk looks kinda suspicious. It's not that cold."

The autumn air was slightly chilly, but she wasn't cold. Or maybe she was just too scared to be aware of the temperature. Following Ray across deserted streets and through unfenced back yards, she persisted in trying to talk him out of going through with his scheme.

"It's Saturday night, Ray. Except for security and the skeleton crews working in the factory, the plant is closed. If anything's going on, it's going on during the day, when Vince and Danielle are there. I'm sure of it."

"I don't think so." Ray motioned her to be quiet

when a dog started to bark. Moving swiftly and silently, he didn't speak again until they reached the base of a hill separating the residential areas from the chemical plant grounds and complex.

"The GC-161 accident happened because the plant was transporting an illegal compound in the daytime," Ray said. "If Danielle Atron hadn't been able to cover it up, it would have caused her and the company a bunch of trouble."

"But she did cover it up, Ray."

"Yeah, but she can't find 'the kid' who got doused with GC-161, and the whole mess has been a major hassle."

Because Alex was "the kid," she was all too aware of the problems the accident had created for everyone. If the transport truck had gone out at night, there wouldn't have been an accident. She would have been home asleep—not walking into the truck's path on the way home from school. She wouldn't have been drenched with the gold compound that had given her strange powers, and she wouldn't be the object of the CEO's relentless search.

"So," Ray concluded, "it makes sense that if the PVC plant is doing something else they shouldn't,

Danielle Atron won't risk ever having anything go wrong in broad daylight again."

"I guess."

"I'm sure. There's less chance of attracting attention at night. And"— Ray paused for emphasis—"no one will be able to see *us* watching *them* in the dark, either."

Another good point, Alex conceded as they started to climb. All of Ray's reasoning was logical. She had to admit she wouldn't be the least bit surprised to learn that the plant was developing other illegal projects. She just didn't want to be the one to find out.

As they neared the top of the hill, Alex pulled the ski mask over her face and dropped to the ground beside Ray. Crawling on their stomachs, they eased up to the crest and looked down on the chemical plant. The grounds were lit up by security lights, and they had an unobstructed view. A few employee cars were parked by the factory entrance, and two guards on foot were patrolling the perimeter fence. Nothing looked out of the ordinary.

"Now what?" Alex hissed in Ray's ear.

Ray pulled two pairs of binoculars out of his

black bag and handed one to Alex. "We watch—and wait."

"Right." Sighing, Alex settled in for a long night. Nothing weird was going to happen at the plant. The only danger they faced was being bored to death—and explaining what they were doing outside in the middle of the night if their parents caught them sneaking back in. She was absolutely positive this adventure was a total waste of time.

And she was right.

Alex woke up in her bed late the next morning, feeling groggy from lack of sleep and sore from lying on the hard ground for five hours.

For nothing.

Well, not exactly for nothing, Alex thought as she dragged herself out of bed. Wincing as she stretched her stiff arms and legs, she wondered if Ray was suffering with similar discomforts. Although he was determined to continue the stakeouts, she was sure he would give up after another night or two. Watching the security guards walk, sit, and check the plant gates was just slightly more exciting than filling in all the O's on a cereal box. Boredom and pain would do more to discourage Ray than any rational argument she could come up with.

After stashing the black clothes under her bed, Alex splashed cold water on her face and went downstairs. Her parents were sitting at the kitchen table, sipping coffee and looking as bleary-eyed as she felt.

"Hi!" Alex said brightly. Her mom and dad both smiled tightly as she sat down and poured a glass of orange juice. They were looking at her strangely, and she wondered if they knew she had sneaked out last night. No, she decided. She had morphed to get back inside without making any noise, and they had both been sound asleep.

"You're up late this morning." Mr. Mack reached for the coffeepot in the center of the table and grimaced. Rubbing his shoulder, he held out his cup for Mrs. Mack to pour.

"Yeah. I guess working in the garage wore me out," Alex said.

"It was sweet of you to offer to clean it, Alex." Mrs. Mack lifted the pot and tipped it. The last dribble of coffee plopped into Mr. Mack's cup. "Guess I'd better make another pot," Barbara Mack said. As she stood up, she bent forward and groaned.

"Are you two okay?" Alex asked.

"Fine," her parents said in unison. Straightening up, Mrs. Mack moaned again and shuffled to the counter.

"So how's your project going?" Mr. Mack shifted position slowly, turning his whole body to face her.

"Slow," Alex admitted. "You were right. It's a big job. I don't think I'll get it all done until next weekend."

"Get what done?" Annie asked as she strolled into the kitchen and dropped her books on the counter.

Startled, Mr. Mack looked up, winced, and rubbed his neck. Mrs. Mack grabbed her back and inhaled sharply as she reached across the counter to plug in the coffeepot. Bewildered, Annie looked back and forth between them.

"I'm cleaning the garage," Alex said.

"Cleaning the garage?" Annie's gaze snapped to Alex. "Why?"

"*Dad* was going to do it, but Mom needed him to help her practice tennis, so I volunteered."

"I see." Sliding into a chair, Annie nodded almost imperceptibly at Alex, to let her know she understood the situation.

"We've got the courts reserved for noon," Mr. Mack said. "If we're going to get there on time, we'd better get moving."

"It's only ten," Annie said, checking her watch. "You've got plenty of time."

"Not at the rate I'm moving this morning." Rising stiffly, Mr. Mack took Mrs. Mack by the arm and they both hobbled out the kitchen door.

"Maybe another hot bath will help," Mrs. Mack muttered, pausing at the bottom of the stairs.

"We could cancel the reservation," Mr. Mack said hopefully.

"No, dear. The only way to get in shape is to work out the kinks. A little limbering up and we'll be fine." Mrs. Mack started upward, slowly, one step at a time.

Annie looked at Alex quizzically. "Tennis?"

"Mom's teamed up with the mayor's wife in a tournament next weekend. She wants to play well, but I think they overdid it yesterday." Yawning, Alex rested her chin in her hand and gave in to her own exhaustion.

"Why are you so tired?"

Alex decided not to tell Annie she was helping Ray investigate the plant for a newspaper story. She knew it was a stupid and dangerous thing to do, but until Ray decided to abandon the midnight watches, he needed her. She wasn't going to change his mind, so there was no reason to subject herself to Annie's arguments against it.

"Cleaning the garage is hard work." Stifling another yawn, Alex briefly explained yesterday's close call.

"That was quick thinking, Alex. Offering to do the job for him was the only way out."

"Yeah, but now we're stuck with it. I promised." Alex wanted to go back to bed when her parents left for the courts, but that would just make Annie suspicious. As tired as she was, it would be better to tackle the project and get it over with.

"What do you mean 'We're stuck with it'?" Annie said. "I can't help you, Alex."

Alex's heavy eyelids popped open. "But Dad was going to clean the garage because *you* didn't straighten up your stuff when he asked!"

"I'm sorry about that, Alex, but I've got a major test tomorrow and two papers to write by Thursday."

"Sorry? That's not enough, Annie. I can't do this without your help. I don't know what's important and what isn't. And if I don't make some progress, Dad might start poking around again. And if he finds the GC-161 stuff—"

"I know, but Bryce is coming over to study for tomorrow's chemistry exam. We both want to ace it with perfect scores."

"This is my *life* we're talking about! If Dad and Mom suspect I'm the kid who was exposed to GC-161, they'll panic. They'll make me go to a doctor and Danielle will find out and—"

"I don't think that's an immediate problem. Dad won't be cleaning anything for a while—he can hardly walk. Trust me. Lugging junk out of the garage is the last thing he'll want to do when he gets home later."

The doorbell rang, and Annie stood up to answer it. "And anyway, as long as it looks like you've accomplished something, he'll be happy. Just start in one spot and be methodical. We've got a week, and I'll help you. But not today." Annie paused in the hall and looked back. "Don't touch any of my stuff."

"I wouldn't dream of it." Sighing, Alex went into the garage and sat down on an overturned milk crate. Surrounded by stacks and piles of stuff, she felt totally overwhelmed.

"Just start in one spot," Annie had said. *Easier*

said than done, Alex thought as she scanned the accumulated chaos. Her gaze settled on the old magazines stacked high on shelves attached to the wall above her. Concentrating, Alex reached out with her thoughts to lift the pile on the end. Too late, she realized that her weary mind had wandered, and she was focused on the shelf instead of the magazines. The telekinetic force pulled the shelf brackets off the wall and ten years' worth of magazines fell into a heap at her feet.

Alex stared at them. Between cleaning the garage for her dad, helping Ray with his investigation, and going to school, it was going to be a very long and exhausting week.

CHAPTER 4

It had taken her all Sunday afternoon to sort a bunch of magazines, stack and tie a ton of newspapers, and stuff a couple of trash bags with almost-empty paint cans. First, she'd had to get an okay from Annie that she wasn't throwing out anything of scientific value. The garage looked worse than it had before Alex started, but her father hadn't checked when he came home. Alex had hoped to grab a nap before she was due to meet Ray, but it was obvious her parents appreciated her being there to help them out. And Annie had gone to Bryce's house to study, away from the distraction of TV and tennis talk. So Alex dutifully heated up leftovers for dinner, cleaned up the kitchen, and even found and handed her father the remote for the TV. He assured her that he had the strength to press the buttons, and at that point Alex wasn't sure if she could muster the energy herself to channel-surf. By then, it was too late for a nap.

Sneaking out hadn't been quite so easy, either. Her parents had retired early again, but Annie had arrived home just before nine. It was after ten before she was sleeping soundly enough for Alex to leave. Ray wasn't happy about the delay and had insisted they jog the entire route to make up for lost time. Then they spent another boring five hours on the hill overlooking the chemical plant. The only break in the monotony was provided by a burned-out bulb in a tall security lamp. Watching the guards struggle with a ladder to change it had been mildly interesting, but hardly worth missing another night's sleep.

By Monday night, Alex was ready to call it quits. She trudged after Ray through a storm of swirling leaves torn from the trees by a cold wind. There was a chance of rain, and the thin sliver of moon peeking through the clouds was not enough to light up the dark. Tired, chilled, and sore to the bone, Alex vowed that this was her last midnight prowl. Her energy reserves were drained, and Ray still didn't have a news story. *He isn't the least bit discouraged, either,* Alex thought glumly as Ray leaped over a split-rail fence and darted ahead. He disappeared into the shadows along the outside edge of a driveway. Alex climbed the three wooden rails, catching her toe on the top one. She fell into a pile of leaves, snapping a buried branch.

A dog started to bark.

Startled, Ray circled back and set off a motion-activated light on the corner of someone's garage. He froze.

Picking herself up, Alex dashed to the garage and zapped the light. A streak of gold electrical energy shot from her fingers, turning off the mechanism. The safety of black night instantly surrounded them again. Grabbing her hand, Ray hauled her toward the street.

"What's the matter with you tonight?" Ray whispered after they had scurried across the pavement and into the yard at the base of the hill.

Brushing bits of leaves off her sweater, Alex whispered back, "I may have powers, Ray, but I'm not superhuman. I'm so tired, I can't stand it.

I actually dozed off during a math test today. I only barely finished before the bell rang."

"Then go home and go to bed. You're the one who wanted to help, Alex. I didn't want you to come with me, remember?"

"Yeah. Sorry. It's just that—" Taking a deep breath, Alex peered up the incline to the crest of the hill. Backlit by the glow of the plant's security lights, the rocks and scrub trees on the ridge looked like ghostly guardians of Danielle Atron's dark secrets. If Ray uncovered something sinister and the CEO found out, he'd be in grave danger. And if something awful happened to Ray because she wasn't there to help, Alex would never forgive herself. Her only other option was to convince him to give up.

Rolling up her ski mask, Alex began: "Taking these risks wouldn't be so bad if we were accomplishing something out here, Ray. But we're not. And it's not that I don't want you to get a scoop about the plant for the *PV Press*. I do. There just doesn't seem to be a scoop to get."

"It kinda looks that way, doesn't it?" Sighing deeply, Ray shook his head. "I was so sure we'd find something bad going on down there at night.

There *is* a story, Alex. I can feel it, but maybe you're right. This isn't the way to get it."

"That's what I think." Alex tried to sound as disappointed as Ray looked. He really wanted to give Mr. Hardwick a hard news story for the paper, and she really wanted to divert the editor's attention from the accident. Still, Mr. Hardwick had been in the newspaper business for years, and he hadn't been able to prove Danielle Atron was doing anything wrong. It was silly to think she and Ray could.

"So maybe we should just go home and forget it," Alex said.

"But we're almost there! It can't hurt to give it one more night. Who knows? Maybe we'll get lucky."

"Ray—"

"If nothing happens tonight, I'll try something different," Ray said solemnly. "Maybe get a job at the plant as a stockboy or something."

"Promise?"

Ray held up his right hand. "Word of honor."

Pulling down her mask, Alex gave in and followed Ray up the hill. When they reached the pile of rocks, she made herself as comfortable as possible. Below, the plant parking lot looked pretty much the same as it had the past two nights. There were a few more cars and four security guards instead of two, but it was Monday. Plant operations were in full swing. Sighing, she settled in for another uneventful watch, but at least it would be the last one.

Alex's eyelids grew heavy and her vision blurred as she stared through her binoculars. The wind blew colder and the night grew darker as clouds covered the thin crescent moon. Except for the guards walking the fence, nothing moved in the parking lot. All she could think about was being home, asleep in a warm bed. . . .

"Alex!"

"Huh? What?" Alex woke up with a start when Ray nudged her. She had dozed off, and it took her a few seconds to remember where she was. Cold raindrops pelted her face and she shivered.

"This is it, Alex!" Ray whispered loudly and bounced with excitement. "It's going down now!"

"What's going down?" Picking up her binoculars, Alex peered below at the plant. The four security guards had taken defensive positions in front of a storage shed a short distance from the factory. Two other men hauled a large yellow barrel out of the shed and loaded it onto a truck that was just like the one Dave had been driving when he almost ran her down two years ago. Then they went back into the shed and came out with a second barrel.

"Think it's GC-161 again?" Ray asked.

"I don't know." Alex squinted through the glasses. "There's writing on the barrels, but I can't read it."

"We should be closer." Ray tapped his fist against the rock in frustration, then leaned forward as the men loaded the second barrel, closed the truck doors, and got into the cab.

"Get down, Ray! Someone might see you."

Ray eased back as the driver started the engine and drove through the gate. He followed the truck with his binoculars until it turned east on Highway 18 and disappeared into the night. Then he lowered the binoculars and grinned.

"We got 'em, Alex!"

"Got what, Ray?" Alex huddled against the rock for protection from the wind and drizzle. "How do we know that truck isn't making a regular delivery?"

"We don't, but I don't believe *that* for a minute." Ray checked the glowing readout on his watch. "It's just after twelve. Who loads regular stuff in the middle of the night?"

"Anyone who wants a delivery to arrive first thing in the morning," Alex countered quickly.

"But they don't load their trucks with security guards covering them." Ray was bursting with excitement and would not even consider that the truck might be transporting ordinary cargo. He raised the binoculars to scan the area around the storage shed again, then stopped suddenly. "And the head of security wouldn't be hanging around to supervise, either."

"Vince is down there?" Alex's heart sank as she peered at the storage shed. Vince walked out of the shadows, checked the time, and said something to the guards. They nodded, then returned to their regular patrols as he disappeared into the administration building. *There's no way out now*, Alex thought miserably. The head of Paradise Valley Chemical security wouldn't be interested in a routine delivery.

"Now what?" Alex asked, dreading the answer.

"Tonight we'll just keep watching to see if and when that truck comes back."

"And then?"

Letting his binoculars hang around his neck,

Ray sat on the ground beside her. He pulled a minirecorder out of his bag. "And then tomorrow night, we'll hide on that ridge behind the shed so we can get a closer look. We've got to find out what's in those barrels."

While Ray dictated his observations into the recorder, Alex worried. If they were captured by plant security, Vince would know they had been spying. Why else would two kids be on the ridge behind the plant with binoculars at midnight? He'd call their parents or maybe even have them arrested, but first he might decide to test them for GC-161. That would be a fate worse than death for her.

But Alex couldn't ignore what she had seen, either. Vince *might* just be working late, and the truck *could* be making a routine delivery. But what if it wasn't? If Danielle Atron was transporting another illegal and harmful chemical, she had to be stopped before someone got hurt. Alex knew that she had been lucky GC-161 hadn't had worse side effects. Somebody else exposed to GC-161 or another experimental chemical might not be so lucky.

Danielle Atron didn't want her benevolent image tainted, so bad publicity in the local paper would probably make her back off from a dangerous project, at least for a while. But Mr. Hardwick needed proof before he could go to press. Without proof, they were just two kids who'd been out playing investigative reporters. After all, no one else knew what Ray and Alex knew about the plant—that it had covered up its last illegal chemical disaster, making it more likely that they were doing it again. And Alex and Ray couldn't say anything about the GC-161 spill, so why would Mr. Hardwick want to investigate?

It all boiled down to one unavoidable conclusion: no one else could go after the story but Alex and Ray.

CHAPTER 5

"It's nine o'clock," Annie said sharply.

Alex groaned and rolled over. Her first thoughts were: *What time is it and what day is it?* Then she remembered it was Wednesday night. Glancing at her alarm clock, she wished it were nine o'clock in the morning, not nine at night. Then she would have had a solid night's sleep. A two-hour after-dinner nap wasn't enough, and she didn't want to get up.

On Monday night, she and Ray had waited for the Paradise Valley Chemical truck to return, which it did only three hours after it left. That meant it hadn't gone out to make a routine morning delivery. On Tuesday night, Alex and Ray had been supercharged with anticipation as they headed for the ridge behind the storage shed. They had hoped to learn something about the cargo, and maybe even the truck's destination, but the plant hadn't sent out another truck. There probably wouldn't be a truck leaving tonight, either, but Ray was determined to keep up the surveillance until there was—even if it took weeks!

Annie shook her. "You wanted me to wake you up, remember?"

"Mm-hmm." Propping herself up on her elbow, Alex rubbed her eyes. Annie was hovering beside the bed with her arms crossed. Alex ignored the questioning frown on her sister's face as she sat up and forced herself awake.

"You've been dragging around the house for days, Alex. Why don't you just sleep?"

There was an edge of challenge in Annie's tone. Alex ignored that, too, and simply said, "Can't."

"Why not?"

"I've got"—Alex couldn't hold back a yawn—"too much to do and not enough time to do it."

Annie nodded as she perched on the bed beside Alex. "I can certainly relate to that. Studying with Bryce Sunday for that chemistry test helped."

"How'd you both do?" Standing up, Alex stretched.

"Almost perfect. I snagged a ninety-nine percent and Bryce ended up with a ninety-seven." Annie fell back with a weary sigh. "But I'm worn out from trying to catch up. At least my papers are almost done. Just a few finishing touches and I can print them out."

"When are they due?" Alex asked casually as she tucked in her shirt and headed for the door.

"Tomorrow." Annie eyed her curiously. "Where are you going?"

"First to the refrigerator, then the garage." Alex was pretty sure Annie didn't suspect she had been sneaking out. Luck had been with her again last night. Annie had been at the library when she left. Then, when she returned home at four o'clock in the morning, she had found Annie asleep at the kitchen table, where she had been working on her history paper. Alex had tiptoed directly to bed without waking her, but her luck was bound to run out soon. After school today, she had put her black clothes in the garage just in case Annie was home and awake tonight. Now all she had to do was keep Annie out of the garage.

"You're going to work in the garage at this hour?" Annie sat up. "Dad hasn't said anything about it, has he?"

"No. He hasn't gone near the garage, just like you said. He's so upset about being stiff and sore after playing a few games of tennis, he's been meeting Mom at the courts after work to get back in shape."

Annie smiled. "I'm sure glad they've got their own bathroom. Mom's practically been living in the tub."

"Yeah, but her game's improving, and they seemed to be moving around better tonight. If she keeps it up, she and Mrs. Lincoln might actually win the tournament. But *after* the tournament, Dad'll forget about tennis and start thinking about the garage again. So I've got to get enough done to keep him satisfied."

Alex paused, wondering if she should ask her sister for help in the garage. Even though Annie was hard pressed to finish her paper, Alex decided to go for it. "I could use some help."

Annie threw up her hands. "Alex, I just can't right now."

"I know." Alex sighed for effect. "I'll do what

I can the next couple of days, but you've *got* to help me this weekend."

"I will," Annie said earnestly. "We'll get it done by the time Mom and Dad get back from Lakewood Sunday night."

"Okay. Thanks." Closing the bedroom door behind her, Alex hurried down the hall. She could hear the water running in her parents' bathroom, so she didn't have to worry about her mom. Her father was doing sit-ups on the living room floor.

"Hey, Alex. Thirty-six, thirty-seven—where have—thirty-eight—you been—thirty-nine—all night? Forty!" Exhaling loudly, Mr. Mack relaxed and grinned.

"Taking a nap. I want to get some more done in the garage tonight."

Rising, Mr. Mack stretched and inhaled deeply. "Well, believe it or not, it seems like the more exercise you get, the more energy you've got. Why don't I give you a hand?"

"No!" Alex blurted, then fumbled for a reason why she didn't want any help. "I—uh, I'm being very systematic about it, Dad, and, umm, it still looks like a disaster even though it really isn't, because I know the system and you don't. And, uh, you're always telling me I've got to finish what I start, right?"

Mr. Mack nodded, then looked confused. "I am?"

"Right. See, I started cleaning the garage, so I want to finish it. By myself."

Mrs. Mack appeared at the top of the stairs wearing a bathrobe and carrying a bundle of laundry. "Would you throw these in the washer, George? It's supposed to warm up tomorrow, but I'd like to have fresh sweats to wear just in case." Mrs. Mack tossed the clothes, threw Alex a kiss, and went back into the bedroom.

Alex scooped them up. "I'll do it, Dad. I'm going to be in the garage for a while anyway, and there's stuff in front of the washer and drier."

"But—"

Alex backed toward the kitchen. "This is just something I've got to do, Dad. Taking responsibility and all that. Thanks for being so understanding."

"Sure." Mr. Mack frowned, then shrugged and said, "Any time."

Alex fled into the garage and locked the door. The clock on the wall read 9:18. She had just enough time to run a wash cycle and get the wet load into the drier before she left to meet Ray.

Shoving one cardboard box away from the front of the washer and lifting another off the top, Alex turned and realized there was no place to put it. She was making about as much progress cleaning as Ray was in his investigation: almost none.

The sorted papers and magazines were piled in the middle of the floor. Trash bags lay in heaps in front of the shelves on the far wall. She had separated the things she thought should be tossed: empty cans and bottles in one bag, broken toys and tools in another, torn and moldy clothes in another, and so on. But she couldn't throw them out until Annie checked them, and they were taking up valuable space.

Setting the box back on the washer, Alex decided to tie the trash bags and set them outside the door. The plastic would protect the contents if it rained again, and they were full of junk anyway. The cardboard boxes held various household and personal items she was pretty sure the family wanted to keep, so they had priority inside. Five minutes later, the washer was clear, and she stuffed the sweats inside and turned it on. Then she hauled trash until it was time to shift the clothes into the drier and change into her black outfit.

Ray, who was pacing in the driveway, jumped when Alex came around the corner of the garage. "Alex!" he said. "Don't scare me like that. My nerves are already maxed out."

"How come? I'm not late."

"Just a feeling," Ray said as he started off down the sidewalk. "Something's going to happen at the plant tonight."

"I hope so." Alex talked as she jogged beside him. "I don't know how much longer I can leave the house for hours in the middle of the night without someone noticing. I think Annie's getting suspicious."

Alex wasn't exactly thrilled with the deception, either. Her parents' rules were made to protect her, and Annie gave her a hard time about using her powers foolishly for the same reason. Sneaking around and deliberately putting herself in danger seemed really stupid. She wasn't sure if protecting Ray and stopping Danielle Atron from hurting someone else was enough to justify her actions.

"Once we know for sure that the plant is up to

no good, Annie will cover for you, Alex," Ray said, as he climbed over a low hedge.

Maybe, Alex thought, *but I don't want to be anywhere near her if she finds out the risk I've been taking.*

Alex put that problem out of her mind as they skirted the base of the hill and climbed the far side to the ridge behind the storage shed. Hiding in a clump of scrub trees, they hunkered down to wait. Alex's heart raced slightly when she realized there were four security guards patrolling the fence. There were also four guards on the night they'd seen the mysterious barrels get hauled away. Ray's hunch might prove right after all.

Just after midnight, a truck drove across the parking lot. The guards surrounded it as it pulled up in front of the shed.

"We're still too far away to hear what they're saying!" Ray fumed as the driver and a second man got out of the truck.

"The light's not good enough to read anything, either." Alex shared Ray's anxious frustration. Seeing the trucks being loaded at midnight under extra security left no doubt in her mind that something bad was going on. "So what do we do?"

Ray took a deep breath and looked at her pointedly. "One of us has to get closer."

Alex nodded and studied the terrain between their position and the fence just beyond the shed. The ridge was steep and covered with loose stones and dry brush, and there were no trees or large rocks to hide behind. Ray couldn't possibly crawl closer without making noise or being seen.

"Guess this is one of those times when my powers will come in handy, huh?"

"No." Ray set his binoculars down. "This is my story, and I'm the one who should take the chances."

Alex touched his arm. "This is too important, Ray. We've got to find out what they're doing, but you don't have a chance of getting down there and back safely. If I morph into a puddle, I can. And we're wasting time arguing about it."

Ray reluctantly agreed.

Concentrating, Alex felt a warm tingle as her cellular structure changed. The heat coursing through her body dissipated as she morphed into liquid form and slithered cautiously out of the trees. The ground was cold and her puddle-self shivered with the chill and fear. Although Ray had not spotted Vince lurking in the shadows, the security guards were on alert and looking for anything suspicious.

Halfway down the ridge, Alex oozed over a bed of round pebbles. She didn't realize this was a mistake until it was too late. Like rushing water churning up the bottom of a riverbed, she dislodged several of the stones. Gravity sent them rolling down the hill just as two men came out of the shed with the first barrel.

"Hold it!" one of the guards barked, and held up his hand. The two men froze.

Alex slid into a cramped crevice between some low, flat rocks as the guards swept the hillside with high-intensity flashlights. She trembled, terrified that the beams of light would find Ray hiding in the trees above.

But it wasn't Ray she had to worry about. The bright beams flashed over the rocks, then zipped back again and stopped. In her morphed state, she was too massive to fit entirely into the narrow crack. The light illuminated the shimmering bulge of her jelly-form, which overlapped the top of the rocks. Alex stiffened.

"What's that?" a guard asked.

"It's hard to tell in the dark, even with a flashlight," another guard said. "It looks like there's some kind of a silvery glob wedged between the rocks."

"Maybe I should check it out," the first guard suggested.

Alex muffled a gurgling cry of alarm. If the guard examined her closely, he might figure a glob of thick, silvery ooze was just a by-product of the chemical plant's manufacturing processes.

However, she could only stay morphed for five minutes. That meant that if the guard took the time to investigate, she would materialize right in front of his eyes!

CHAPTER 6

"Forget it." The second guard turned off his flashlight. "It's just a piece of trash or something, and we've got a schedule to keep."

Alex, in her jelly state, relaxed with a soft, squishing sound. Then, worried that the guards heard the noise, she froze again. But the men didn't react.

"Guess you're right." The first guard sighed. "Vince wants that stuff dumped and the truck back before daylight."

"And if we mess up this operation tonight, he'll stick around Friday to make sure we don't mess up again," a third man said.

"So we'd better not mess up," the fourth guard

added sternly. "The less I see of the boss, the more I like it."

All the guards muttered in agreement and switched off their flashlights.

Alex eased out of the crevice and under a bush by the fence. She was anxious to get back to Ray.

"Okay, Bart," the first guard said impatiently. "Get those barrels loaded and move on out of here."

"You heard the man, Sam." The driver motioned to his partner, and they hoisted the large yellow barrel into the truck.

Alex muffled another gasp as she read the words stenciled on the side of the container:

TOXIC WASTE

EXTREMELY HAZARDOUS MATERIALS

DO NOT OPEN

Alex didn't wait for the men to load the second barrel. She had found out everything she could, and she had less than a minute left before she would materialize. Gliding silently and swiftly, she zoomed upward over the rough ground.

She almost made it.

Ten feet from the trees and safety, a pulsing

warmth rushed through her liquefied cells. She materialized within seconds, heard Ray gasp, and dropped to the ground. Heart pounding, she looked down the hill. The driver was closing the truck doors, and the guards were watching him. She hadn't been seen.

Once again her luck was holding, but this time Alex decided not to push it to the limit. Lying flat on the ground, she waited. When the truck was out the gate and the guards had resumed their normal patrols, she belly-crawled back into the trees where Ray was waiting.

"Man, that was close." Ray heaved a long sigh of relief, then nodded toward the back side of the hill. "Let's get out of here."

"Right behind you," Alex said. Tense and breathless from running, neither one of them spoke until they were off the plant's property and headed home through the now familiar back yards.

Ray broke the silence. "Well, tonight sure wasn't dull. I don't think I could have taken much more of watching nothing."

"To be honest, there were a couple of times on that hill when watching nothing didn't seem quite so bad to me."

"Tell me about it. When those guards had their lights shining on you, I was getting ready to create a diversion so you could get away."

"Then they would have caught you, Ray!"

Ray shrugged. "Better me than you. The worst they could do to me is have me arrested and thrown in the clink until my dad came to get me. But if they had seen you change from a puddle of silver gunk into a girl, you'd be in Danielle Atron's lab right now . . . and you'd never get out."

Alex shuddered. "I'm glad you didn't have to do anything that drastic, but it's nice to know you were willing to go to jail to save me. Thanks," she said, sending Ray an appreciative smile.

"Don't mention it. What distracted them anyway?"

"They thought I was a piece of garbage or something." Alex almost giggled, then she remembered the other reason the guards had forgotten about her. "And they were afraid of getting in trouble with Vince if they messed up the delivery."

Ray slapped his forehead. "I was so worried about you and getting away, I got totally spaced about *why* we went up there. Some reporter." Jogging ahead, Ray jumped the split-rail fence and walked on with his head hanging.

Alex vaulted the rails and caught up to him. "Actually, you're a good reporter, Ray. Your hunch was right. The plant is dumping toxic waste."

"They are?" Ray stopped on the sidewalk. "What kind of toxic waste?"

"The barrels just said 'extremely hazardous materials,' " Alex recalled.

"Where are they dumping it?"

"I don't know that, either, but Vince definitely doesn't want anyone to find out. That's why they're making the runs in the middle of the night."

"Then it's got to be somewhere illegal." Ray's smile faded as he realized just how serious the situation was. "What if they're putting that stuff where it could contaminate people's homes or a school or something?"

"Exactly what I was thinking." Alex sighed.

"The only thing we know for sure is that the location is about an hour and a half away from here because it took the truck three hours to get back the other night," Ray recalled. "But that could be in any direction."

"The truck went east on Highway 18 again tonight."

"Oh, yeah. East." Ray tapped his chin. "Highway 18 goes into the mountains."

"It's not our problem anyway, Ray. Mr. Hardwick will know how to find out where and stop it."

"I can't go to Mr. Hardwick with this yet, Alex. We've got to find out where they're dumping *first.*" Frowning thoughtfully, Ray darted across the street.

Stunned by this unexpected development, Alex dashed after him. "Why can't we tell your editor?"

"For one thing, we're *assuming* the dumping is illegal. What if the plant *isn't* doing anything wrong?"

Alex slowed as they approached her house. "I don't understand."

"I couldn't look Mr. Hardwick in the eye ever again if I sent him on a wild goose chase that made him look dumb in front of Danielle Atron and the whole town."

"No, I guess not." *If that happens,* Alex thought, *Mr. Hardwick might just become more determined to investigate the GC-161 accident to save his wounded pride and reputation.* And that wouldn't be good for her, either.

Sagging, Alex asked the next logical question that came to mind. "How are we gonna follow a truck?"

"Good question. We can't keep up on our bikes, but I'll think of something by tomorrow night."

"Actually, we can sleep tomorrow night. They're not making another run until Friday. That's what I heard the guards say."

"Excellent. That'll give me more time to solve the problem." As Alex turned into her driveway, Ray paused and glanced at his watch. "You can start catching up on your sleep tonight. It's only one-thirty."

"That's something, I guess." Waving, Alex trudged toward the side door into the garage. Ray had a reasonable argument for everything, but she was too tired to worry about the next phase of his investigation right now. All she wanted to do was fall into bed and go to sleep.

Alex was so exhausted she was halfway across the garage before she realized she wasn't alone. Stopping by the stacks of magazines, she turned to see Annie sitting on a stool, glaring at her.

Alex sighed with weary defeat.

Her luck had just run out.

CHAPTER 7

On Friday afternoon, Alex raced home from school. It had been a tense couple of days, but she felt rested for the first time in a week. Robyn and Nicole were upset because she seemed to be avoiding them, but they had accepted cleaning the garage as an explanation.

And her luck hadn't turned sour, after all. Annie hadn't told their parents what Alex had been doing at night. However, after listening to her explanations and Ray's arguments, Annie still hadn't decided whether to help them. She didn't want to break her Friday-night date with Bryce and she thought Alex had already taken too many foolish risks.

But everything depended on Annie.

They couldn't follow the truck unless Annie agreed to drive her mother's car. No one else could do it. No one else could be trusted to honor Ray's exclusive on the story and keep it secret. And more important, no one else knew about Alex's powers, which she might have to use if they got into a tight spot.

"Annie!" Alex ran inside and almost tripped over the bags and tennis gear stacked by the front door. *Another stroke of incredible luck,* she thought as she dropped her backpack on the couch and went into the kitchen. Her parents had already packed so they'd be ready to leave as soon as they got home from work. Even though the Lakewood Country Club was less than a two-hour drive away, they had decided to stay at a nearby hotel for the weekend instead of commuting back and forth. Her mom would get more rest and practice for the tournament that way. Their absence would make taking the car and staying out until the wee hours of the morning a lot less complicated.

If Annie agreed.

"Annie!" Alex grabbed an apple from a bowl on the counter.

"Out here!" Annie yelled from the garage.

Alex turned the knob on the garage door and tried to push, but something prevented it from opening all the way. She stuck her head in and saw a stack of boxes taller than her in front of the door. Then she stared at the garage in disbelief. It looked like a tornado had hit it. All of Alex's piles and bags and boxes had been turned upside down, as if a bulldozer had come through and turned it into the town dump.

"What are you doing?" Alex wailed.

"Sorting through my equipment. What does it look like?" Annie tossed a broken beaker into a trash bag.

"This is hopeless. It gets worse every day instead of better. We'll never get done by Sunday night." Leaning against the drier, Alex took a bite of the apple.

"We won't if you're just going to stand there stuffing your face. Get busy." Annie pointed to the newspapers and magazines. "You can start by taking those to the curb. I put the keepers back on the shelf."

"Thanks." Alex set the apple on the drier and picked up one of the tied stacks. "What about tonight?"

Annie continued to thumb through a notebook, saying, "I haven't—"

Just then, Ray burst in through the side door. "Okay, Annie. I need a decision. Are you gonna drive?"

"—decided yet." Annie stuffed the notebook into a cardboard box with several others, then whirled to face them. "You two are just asking for trouble, you know that?"

"We're not the ones dumping toxic waste," Ray said. "Seems to me that Danielle Atron's the one asking for trouble."

"*If* she's dumping it illegally," Annie countered hotly.

"Right." Crossing his arms, Ray met her stubborn stare. "And we won't know that until we know where that truck is going. I gotta get this story, Annie. Are you in or not?"

"I don't care about your story, Ray." Annie slumped and rubbed her temples. "But I do care about Alex. I don't want your editor asking questions about the GC-161 accident, and I don't want anyone else getting hurt because Danielle Atron doesn't care."

Alex held her breath and Ray leaned forward expectantly.

"So I'll think about it," Annie finished.

Alex knew that pressing Annie to make up her mind was pointless. She'd decide when she was ready and not before. They could only hope she'd decide to cooperate.

For the next two hours, Ray helped Alex cart trash to the curb and shift boxes under Annie's direction. When Mrs. Mack called them outside to give them last-minute instructions before leaving for the tournament, the garage looked like they had just moved the whole mess to one side.

No surprise, Alex thought as she joined Annie and Ray on the front porch. That's exactly what they had done. It wasn't much of an improvement, but it gave them space to work.

"You sure you'll be all right?" Mrs. Mack asked anxiously.

"We'll be fine," Annie said with an edge of exasperation. "Don't worry, and have a good time."

"Okay." Mrs. Mack turned to leave, then turned back. She slapped her car keys into Annie's hand. "Just in case there's an emergency or something. There won't be, I'm sure, but you've got the number of the hotel, right?"

"It's by the phone," Alex said. "Dad looks a

little anxious, Mom. You'd better get going so you have time for a nice dinner and a good night's sleep before the big match tomorrow."

The three of them stood in the driveway waving until the car turned out of sight at the end of the block. Then Alex snatched the keys from Annie's hand.

"Alex! Give those back!" Annie grabbed for the keys.

"Nope." Alex telekinetically dangled the keys in the air just out of Annie's reach. "Are you driving? Or am I?"

"You wouldn't dare, Alex Mack."

"You're right. I wouldn't." Alex sighed and let the keys drop to the ground. "We really need you, Annie."

Annie picked up the keys and stared at them. "I suppose if I don't drive, you'll try to follow them anyway."

"That's a definite possibility," Alex said.

"Yeah." Ray nodded emphatically. "Maybe Alex could morph and hide in the truck."

Alex eagerly nodded back. "What a great idea!" She knew that would get Annie worried about her, which was just what she wanted.

Annie glared at them and growled, "All right!

I'll drive!" Then she turned and stomped toward the house.

Ray grinned. "That solves one problem."

"Yeah." Alex's elation at winning Annie over waned quickly as the reality of what they'd all just decided sank in.

They were going to follow a plant truck that might be illegally dumping toxic waste out in the middle of nowhere in the middle of the night. If something went wrong, no one would know where to look for them or what had happened to them.

Their problems, Alex realized grimly, were just beginning.

CHAPTER 8

"There it is." Ray lowered his binoculars as the truck rolled toward the chemical plant gate. Sitting in the front seat of the Macks' car, he looked back and gave Alex a thumbs-up. Alex looked out the side window and saw the truck exiting the grounds of the complex. There were two men riding in it.

"I just know I'm going to regret this," Annie muttered. Her knuckles turned white as she tightened her grip on the steering wheel. Annie had parked in a dark driveway off the highway. They could see the gate, but their car was hidden by brush and trees. They were all dressed in black, and a tangle of branches overhead blocked the light from the crescent moon.

As the truck turned onto the highway, Alex tensed. Everyone ducked until it roared past, gaining speed as it headed east.

"Okay! Let's go!" Ray checked his seatbelt and settled back, eager for the chase.

Annie turned the ignition key, then hesitated before firing up the engine.

"What's wrong?" Alex asked anxiously. If the car broke down, they'd have a lot of explaining to do.

"It's so dark," Annie said, peering through the windshield. "I won't be able to see the road unless the lights are on. They're going to know we're following them."

"All they'll know is that there's a car behind them," Ray said. "This is the main road into the mountains and everybody uses it."

"I hope you're right." Starting the engine, Annie shifted into gear, eased the car to the end of the driveway, and paused to make sure the way was clear.

Alex glanced up the road. The truck's red tail-lights disappeared around a curve. "Step on it, Annie! We're going to lose them!"

"If we get into an accident, we won't catch them, either!" Annie replied hotly. She leaned forward over the steering wheel and looked both ways.

Ray dropped his forehead into his hand.

Alex sighed helplessly. Annie had finally passed her driver's test, but she still wasn't very confident on the road. Like most new drivers, she was overcautious. Ordinarily, Alex was glad, but tonight timing could mean the difference between success and failure. Gripping the armrest, Alex was suddenly thrown back as Annie turned on the headlights and the car shot out onto the highway.

"Go get 'em, Annie!" Ray grinned as Annie accelerated to the legal speed limit.

After strapping herself into the middle seatbelt, Alex focused on the road ahead. Now that they were actually tracking the plant truck, she was more nervous than ever. They were not playing a spy game any longer; this was for real. If the plant was dumping toxic waste illegally, the two men in the truck knew it. And they might do anything to prevent three kids from finding out and reporting their activities to the authorities.

Annie maintained a discreet distance and kept the taillights in sight most of the time. Forty-five minutes later, the truck turned off the highway onto a secondary paved road at the base of the mountain range.

"It's turning!" Ray and Alex said in unison.

"I know." Rolling her eyes, Annie slowed the car. When the truck vanished around a curve, she turned left to follow. "I have to hang back and hope they don't notice we're still behind them."

"Why?" Ray asked. "This is a mountain road."

"But it's not the route into the resort areas. This is total wilderness." Annie grimaced as the car rattled over a series of potholes. "Don't worry. They won't get too far ahead. This road has more holes than Mom's tennis racket and it winds a lot."

"We'd better keep a sharp lookout, Alex, just in case the truck turns off again," Ray warned.

Nodding, Alex pressed her face against the left window in back, while Ray watched to the right. The road got rougher and steeper as they drove deeper into the forested mountains.

"Lose the lights!" Ray hissed.

Annie hit the control and darkness enveloped them. She braked, stopping the car in the middle of the road, and asked, "What's wrong?"

Ray pointed through the windshield. Red tail-lights glowed faintly off to the right for an instant before being swallowed by the dark. Driving blind, Annie slowly eased the car ahead until Ray spotted a rutted dirt track leading into the woods. The bottom of the car scraped the center hump as Annie turned the wheels into the deep ruts to follow the truck.

"Did we break something?" Annie asked.

"No. We're fine," Ray said. "Just go slow."

"You're doing great, Annie." Alex patted Annie's shoulder. Her eyes had adjusted to the dim moonlight and she watched the side of the track, guiding Annie's steering when she started to drift too far one way or the other.

"I'll never complain about city traffic again," Annie mumbled.

They rode in silence for five minutes, teeth clenched and muscles tensed as the car rocked and jolted over rocks and the uneven ground. Annie slowed when they came to a fork in the track. On the right, Alex saw the truck's red brake lights flash as it topped a rise and started down the other side. Annie pulled into the left fork.

"What are you doing?" Ray demanded.

"Parking," Annie explained bluntly. "We're going to follow on foot the rest of the way. We can walk faster than they're driving right now."

"She's right," Alex said. "There's less chance of being spotted on foot. And we'll make less noise, too."

Pulling the car to the right, Annie began to execute a three-point turn. "If we have to get out of here in a hurry, I want to be pointed in the right direction."

"Good thinking," Ray said. Unfastening his seatbelt, he put his binoculars into his black bag.

As Annie pulled the car out of the turn, she steered too far toward the right, into the soft, muddy earth at the edge of the forest. Alex grabbed the back of the front seat as the car tilted slightly and stopped. Annie gunned the engine. The tires spun, but the car didn't move.

Ray rolled down his window and looked out. "It's practically a swamp out there."

"You mean we're stuck?" Annie asked, aghast.

"For the moment." Shouldering his bag, Ray opened his door and leaped, trying to avoid the swampy ground.

Alex and Annie scrambled out the other side.

"What are we going to do?" Shaking her head, Annie walked to the front of the car and looked at the embedded wheel.

"Worry about it later," Ray said. "Right now

74

we've got to catch up to that truck. That's what we came out here for."

"I second that motion." Alex scanned the dark woods on both sides, then looked toward the fork. "Personally, I don't want to stand here in the middle of the road talking about it. That truck could come back any minute, and we can't be seen."

"Point taken." Annie shivered and zipped up her jacket. "Those guys could be anywhere."

Putting his finger to his lips for silence, Ray led the way. He cut through the woods to the other track and followed it to the top of the rise. The road curved sharply to the left at the bottom of a steep incline. They couldn't see the truck, but muffled voices and clunking sounds drifted upward through the trees. Ray ducked into the woods again.

Alex followed behind Annie, carefully easing around trees and over fallen logs, but it was impossible to move without making noise. Dry leaves rustled and twigs cracked under her feet. A dislodged stone clattered down a slanted, flat rock.

Annie almost ran into Ray when he stopped suddenly. "What's wrong now?" she whispered.

Ray dropped to one knee and ran his hand over

the ground. "Deer trail," he said. "We're in luck." He picked up the pace as he followed the hard-packed path.

Alex was impressed with Ray's newly revealed tracking talents. He had always complained when his dad sent him to summer camp for a month when they were in grade school. Apparently, he had learned a lot more than he had ever let on.

Eventually, the thin moon became visible through a break in the trees. Slowing, Ray crept forward in a crouch. The deer trail continued on down the mountainside, but he ducked toward the open space in the woods. Mimicking his movements, Alex and Annie fell on their stomachs and inched out onto a high ridge overlooking a small lake.

The truck was parked close to the water. One of the yellow barrels sat in the middle of a row-boat, which was tied to a big log on the narrow beach. The driver lifted an oar and fitted it into a metal socket.

"Not hard to figure out what he's planning to do," Ray whispered. "I wonder who owns this land."

"You can check the county records to find out," Alex suggested. Then she shuddered. The plant was putting dangerous chemical by-products into the remote mountain lake. It was a beautiful lake, nestled in the mountains and reflecting the moon. If one of the barrels leaked, the contamination probably wouldn't affect a populated area. But the hazardous waste would kill all the wildlife that lived in or drank from the water.

"Where's the second guy?" Annie asked, scanning the shoreline.

A branch snapped in the woods behind them.

"What's that?" Alex stiffened, certain that the missing man had circled around behind them.

"A clumsy animal, I guess." Relaxing, Annie pointed toward the lake. "The other guy's down there."

Alex just nodded, willing her racing heart to calm down as she watched the second man stumble across the beach. Metal clanged as he dropped something heavy into the boat.

"What are they doing?" Alex whispered.

Ray zeroed in with his binoculars. "Weights. The guy in the boat is attaching weights to the barrels."

"To make sure they sink and stay sunk," Annie said.

The second man untied the boat and jumped

into it after he shoved it into the water. The driver then rowed to the center of the lake, where they dumped the yellow barrel overboard. They didn't start back until the barrel sank.

"I vote we get out of here now," Annie whispered. "It'll take them a while to dispose of the other barrel, and we still have to get the car unstuck."

"But—" Ray started to protest.

"We got what we came for, Ray," Alex said. She suddenly had the uneasy feeling that they were being watched. Nerves, she decided. "If those guys finish their dumping and catch us before we're back on the road, you won't get the story to press. Danielle will find a way to stop you and Mr. Hardwick. You know it as well as I do."

Ray didn't press the issue. Scrambling backward off the rocky ledge, he started back down the deer trail with Annie and Alex on his heels. Their feet thudded softly on the hard-packed ground, and they didn't speak as they wove their way through the thick, dark woods. Alex couldn't tell one twist and turn of the trail from another and wondered if Ray remembered where they'd left the road and entered the trees. If he didn't,

they could end up wandering around the mountain forest for days before anyone found them—
if anyone found them. There didn't seem to be another person around for miles.

Quite suddenly Alex realized she'd been mistaken.

They were not alone.

She brought her hand up to her mouth and muffled a startled scream.

A dark figure had just jumped out of the woods to block their path.

CHAPTER 9

"What are you doing on our land?" a young voice demanded. "And why were you watching those men pollute the water?"

Stunned by the abrupt appearance of the teenage boy, no one said anything for a moment. Alex studied him in the dim moonlight filtering through the trees. His black hair was cut short and he was wearing jeans, a leather jacket over a dark turtleneck, and western-style boots. He watched them suspiciously, his mouth set in a grim line.

"You own this land?" Ray asked.

"My people do, and you're trespassing," the boy replied.

"We apologize for that," Annie said, "but shouldn't you be more concerned about the men dumping chemicals into your lake?"

The boy sighed. "The tribe doesn't own the lake. The reservation boundary runs along the ridge."

"Who does own the lake?" Alex asked bluntly. The Native American boy didn't seem as threatening once he began talking.

"Paradise Valley Chemical owns the lake and several acres surrounding it," he informed them.

"Great." Ray huffed and shook his head. "There goes my story."

"What story?" the boy asked curiously.

"I was going to write an exposé for the *Paradise Valley Press* about how the plant is illegally dumping toxic waste. But if the company owns the land, the dumping isn't illegal, is it?"

"It is if there's any chance the contamination will spread." The boy stared at the ground, deep in thought for a moment. An almost smile tugged at the corners of his mouth when he looked up. "I think we should talk—"

Ray spoke up, filling in the silent blank. "I'm Ray Alvarado. And this is Alex Mack and her sister, Annie."

"Nathan Riverwind." He shook hands all around.

Annie glanced back over her shoulder, and then said, "Would anyone mind if we continue this discussion while we're trying to get the car out of that swamp? I really don't want to hang around here any longer than necessary."

"I'll give you a hand," Nathan offered. He talked as he took the lead through the woods.

Alex listened with a mounting sense of fury as Nathan told them about Danielle Atron's callous disregard for the wilderness and the rights of others. The river that ran through the reservation flowed out of the lake. If the lake became contaminated, the river would be poisoned, too. Nathan's tribe was trying to have the dumping legally stopped, but the plant's lawyers were making sure the process dragged on in the courts. It could be years before the issue was settled. By then, a leak in one of the barrels could cause irreversible damage to the fish and water in the river. Even if Danielle Atron lost the case, it would be too late.

When they reached the car, Nathan began gathering sticks and bark and placing them in front of the tires that were stuck in the swamp. The others pitched in until there was enough to provide traction for the tires.

"There must be some way to stop the plant," Alex insisted as she dropped an armful of branches.

"I wish there was, Alex," Nathan said, "but we've tried everything. The tribe even offered to buy the land, but Danielle Atron refuses to sell. Tossing those barrels into a lake is a lot cheaper than using a safer dump site."

"The profit margin is always the bottom line," Annie said, brushing her dirty hands on her jeans. "The cheap way out always seems to cost more in the end, though."

"Why doesn't your tribe just get the barrels out of the lake?" Ray asked.

"We could, but what would we do with them? We can't afford to have that toxic stuff processed. Besides, Danielle Atron threatened to arrest any member of the tribe she caught trespassing." Nathan frowned, then grinned in amusement. "Guess she didn't appreciate my grandfather's warning."

"Your *grandfather* threatened the plant CEO?" Alex was impressed that an old man had the courage to challenge Danielle Atron. "How did he do it?"

"With the trickster coyote," Nathan said.

Ray blinked. "The what?"

"It's an old myth many of the western tribes have in common. The trickster coyote uses pranks to get revenge for injustices." Nathan shrugged. "What can I say? The elders were desperate, and my grandfather's the tribe shaman. It seemed like a good idea at the time."

"A shaman?" Raymond asked. "You mean like a medicine man?"

Nathan nodded. "You got it, and it's a tough job these days. My grandfather really has faith in the ancient myths and tries to get our people to honor the old traditions, but not enough of us believe in that stuff anymore."

"Like you?" Alex asked.

"I live in the same world you do," Nathan said bluntly. "I drive a car, watch cable TV, read books, and go to school. Some of us don't believe a mythical creature like the trickster coyote will come to our rescue. My friends and I—we don't believe in magic."

Alex looked at Ray sharply. His eyes widened and she knew he had come up with the same idea that had just popped into her own head. Magic and tricksters and pranks . . . *Hmm*, Alex thought. *This situation might not be so hopeless after all. Not with my superpowers.*

"To be honest," Nathan said sadly. "I wish there really was a trickster coyote—not only to save the river, but to save my grandfather's pride, too. Obviously, the coyote has not appeared to avenge us or the land, and that chemical plant woman thinks my grandfather is just a silly old man."

"I lost my wallet," Ray blurted out, patting his back pockets.

Alex took the hint. "It probably fell out back there on the ridge, Ray."

"You don't have time to go back and get it now." Annie looked back and forth between them. "We've got to get out of here before those guys leave!"

"If those men follow their normal routine, they won't be leaving for another half-hour," Nathan said. "I've been watching them all week, and they always take a break between barrels. We can have the car back on the road by the time you find the wallet and get back."

"No time to waste then," Alex said. "Let's go, Ray."

Instead of taking the deer trail to the ridge, Alex and Ray crossed the dirt track and moved into the trees. Walking as quickly and silently as possible, they picked their way down the incline and paused on the edge of the woods fifty yards away from the parked truck. The two men were rowing back from the middle of the lake.

Ray crouched behind a small evergreen and parted the branches to see better. "What are you going to do?" he whispered to Alex.

"Avenge the river and Nathan's grandfather." Alex grinned. "And have a little fun, too."

"Be careful," Ray replied.

Alex morphed and gurgled a reply. "I will."

Oozing between rocks and over piles of fallen branches and leaves, Alex glided silently toward a huge boulder by a front fender of the truck. She materialized, crouching behind the big rock, and waited. Finally one of the men jumped out of the boat and began pulling it through the shallow water to the beach. Throwing a force field around the boat, Alex smiled as the man in the water was yanked to an abrupt halt.

"What's the matter?" the other man asked.

"It's stuck!" The wading man hauled on the tow line, but the boat refused to move.

The second man got out to help him. "Must be hung up on a rock or something." Both men pulled, straining on the rope as they put all their weight into the effort.

Now. Alex disengaged the force field and smothered a giggle. The boat shot forward and both men fell in the water. Sputtering, they stood up and quickly hauled the boat onto the shore. After tying it to a fallen tree, they hurried toward the truck.

She knew it wasn't fair to use her powers to pull pranks on people, but this time the cause was just. She didn't want to hurt the men, just scare them off. They were only doing their jobs and following Vince's orders.

And now for my next trick, Alex thought gleefully.

The shore was littered with small stones. Using telekinesis, Alex sent them rolling down the slightly sloping beach.

"What!" The men jumped and struggled to keep their footing on the moving stones.

"I've got a really bad feeling about this," the

driver said as he scrambled to the back of the truck.

"It's downright spooky." The other man watched the stones roll into the water as he backed toward the passenger side of the cab. "I don't like it."

"Me neither. Let's get out of here." The driver yanked open his door.

Alex zapped the fender and sent an electrical charge into the starter. The truck's engine roared to life. Both men froze.

"How'd that happen?" The driver hesitated, afraid to get into the truck.

The second man stared at him from the opposite side of the cab. "Maybe there's some truth to that silly legend Vince was telling me about."

"What legend is that?" the driver asked.

"Some old medicine man told the boss that if she didn't stop dumping stuff in the lake, this coyote thing was gonna get her."

Alex rattled the tree branches overhanging the truck.

And Ray howled from his hiding place in the trees.

Both men jumped inside the cab.

"Better her than us," the driver said. "If Danielle and Vince want a load dumped tomorrow night, they can do it themselves. *I'm* not coming back here."

Yes! Grinning, Alex watched from behind the rock as the driver spun the wheels on the gravel, then drove off in a cloud of dust and grit.

When the truck disappeared over the rise, Ray walked out of the woods. "That was fantastic, Alex! I thought I was going to burst, I was laughing so hard."

"The howl was a nice touch, too." Alex gave him a high-five.

"Those guys won't be back," Ray said, shaking with laughter.

"They won't, but Vince might," Alex said seriously. "The driver said another run is scheduled for tomorrow night, and I doubt Vince will believe that a mythical coyote played those tricks."

When Alex and Ray got back, the car was parked in the middle of the track and Annie and Nathan were sitting on the hood.

"So . . ." Annie said with a pointed stare at Alex. "Can you explain why those guys just raced down the road like they were running the Indianapolis 500?"

"Did they see you?" Alex said, ignoring her sister's question.

Nathan shook his head. "I don't think so. It's pitch dark over here and they were going too fast to do anything but watch the road in front of them. What did you do?"

"Me?" Alex blinked innocently. "Not much, but your people shouldn't give up on the trickster coyote just yet."

Annie wasn't fooled for a second. "You didn't—"

"Didn't what?" Nathan frowned, looking totally confused.

"Nothing." Annie sighed with resignation, then looked slyly at her sister. "We *did* hear a coyote howl," she said.

Nathan's gaze flicked over them. "You don't think the trickster coyote . . ." He shook his head and said, "No way. That's just a bogus myth."

"Don't be too sure about that, Nathan." Ray nodded knowingly, with a quick look at Alex. "Some pretty strange and unbelievable things happen sometimes that completely defy logic."

That's certainly true, Alex thought, trying to hide her grin.

Nathan paused thoughtfully, then stared into

the forest with a wistful, faraway look in his dark eyes.

"The plant is planning to dump again tomorrow night," Alex said. "And there's a good chance Vince will be making the run."

Annie frowned. "It doesn't matter what those guys tell him, Vince won't be scared off."

"So what do we do?" Nathan asked. "They've already dumped six barrels into the lake. Maybe more."

An unspoken alliance had been formed between the three of them and Nathan, Alex realized. And she was committed to doing whatever she could to save the lake.

"Well, for starters, I think your grandfather should visit Danielle Atron again tomorrow," Alex suggested. "After what happened tonight, the CEO might change her mind."

"And if she doesn't?" Nathan asked.

Alex smiled mysteriously. "Then tomorrow night the trickster coyote will strike again."

CHAPTER 10

"Whoa, Ray. Slow down," Alex said. "You can't give the story to Mr. Hardwick this morning." Alex rummaged through a cardboard box full of broken hardware looking for usable nails. She and her sister and Ray had begun to attack the garage bright and early this Saturday.

"Why not?" Balancing a box on his shoulder, Ray started up the stepladder.

"Because if he prints it in the evening edition, Vince might cancel tonight's dumping run and change the schedule." Annie pointed as Ray slid the box onto a shelf attached to the wall. "Put it in the other corner," she instructed.

Ray shoved the box over and stepped down. "I

thought we *wanted* the plant to stop putting stuff in that lake."

"We do." Alex snapped plastic lids onto coffee cans filled with assorted nails, screws, and bolts. "But we want them to stop forever, not just until the bad publicity blows over. If Nathan's grandfather can't convince Danielle Atron to stop dumping those chemicals in the lake, we'll have to convince Vince."

Annie handed Ray another box. "And to do that, we have to *know* that a truck is going out so Alex can prepare. So let's not jeopardize their trucking schedule. It'll take more than rolling rocks and rattling branches to scare Vince off."

"That makes sense, but what if Vince doesn't show?" Ray asked. "He's the head of security at PVC, not a truck driver." Ray moved up the ladder again.

"He'll get Dave to drive," Annie said, "but Vince will be there. Count on it. I don't think he'll be able to resist checking out the other driver's story. Even if it's just to prove that they're wimps and he's not."

"I bet he thinks that Nathan's people pulled the pranks that spooked those guys," Alex added.

"And since Danielle Atron ordered them to stay

off her property, Vince will want to catch them red-handed so he can have them arrested," Annie said, holding on to the ladder to steady it. "That's a power trip he won't pass up."

The box started to fall as Ray put his hand on the wall to keep his balance. Alex telekinetically grabbed the box and eased it into position.

Just then, the phone and doorbell both rang.

"You get the phone, Alex. I'll get the door," Annie said.

As Annie dashed past on her way to the front door, Alex picked up the phone and said, "Hello." Robyn was on the other end of the line.

"The mall is having a huge sidewalk sale today. Nicole and I thought we'd check it out, then catch a movie. Wanna go?"

"I'd love to, but I can't," Alex said, with regret in her voice. She hadn't spent any time with Robyn and Nicole outside school all week because of her promise to clean the garage. And during school, she had been a walking zombie after watching the plant through half the night.

Robyn hesitated. "Are you sure you're not mad at us or something? You've been acting really weird lately."

"Alex!" Annie called from the living room. "Would you come here, please?"

Alex tried to sound calm and convincing—she hated keeping things from her friends. "No, I'm not mad," she said sincerely. "I still haven't finished the garage, and I promised my dad I'd take care of it this weekend. Gotta go. I'll call you tomorrow. 'Bye."

"What's Annie yelling about?" Ray asked as he grabbed a bag of chips off the counter and fell into step behind Alex.

Shrugging, Alex ran into the living room. Nathan Riverwind was sitting on the couch with a white-haired man wearing a three-piece suit and tie.

"This is Nathan's grandfather, Mr. Riverwind," Annie said.

"Glad to meet you." Alex shook the man's hand and shifted uncomfortably under his scrutinizing gaze. With his short hair and business clothes, he didn't look like her idea of a tribal shaman. And yet, his dignified bearing and piercing stare gave her the unsettling impression that he possessed a powerful and ancient wisdom.

The old man nodded, acknowledging Ray, then

looked at Alex. "My grandson tells me you and this young man called on the trickster coyote to help us—and he listened." His dark eyes were mischievously bright within the folds of his stern, wrinkled face.

"Well, sort of," Alex said, frantically trying to come up with a reasonable explanation. "We, uh, just played a few tricks of our own, actually. The plant drivers must have thought it was the coyote."

The old man nodded again but said nothing.

"Nathan and Mr. Riverwind just came from Danielle Atron's office." Annie paced in front of the fireplace.

"What happened?" Ray asked.

Nathan shook his head with disgust. "She laughed and had some guy called Vince escort us out of the plant. He said he wasn't afraid of our ridiculous myths and we wouldn't be able to run him off with our pathetic pranks. He told us to stay off the land surrounding the lake. And that if we tried to interfere in the plant's business again, he'd make us pay."

"The lake belongs to Paradise Valley Chemical," Nathan's grandfather said. "The law is on their side."

"All is not lost. There are certain forces that just might intervene," Annie said with a determined glance at Alex. "I think we can help you."

"I don't see how." Nathan's shoulders sagged in defeat.

"You'll just have to trust us on that one," Ray said.

"We cannot allow you to get into trouble with these chemical plant people," the old man said. "It's our fight."

Alex couldn't tell the old man that they were *already* in big trouble with the chemical plant people. GC-161 had drastically changed her life, and the side effects of the experimental compound could have been a lot worse. Treating toxic chemicals in a careless way was dangerous. So as far as Alex was concerned, it was her fight, too.

"They didn't tell *us* to stay off their property," Alex countered. "And there aren't any No Trespassing signs posted around the lake. The worst that can happen is Vince will think we're a bunch of kids using the lake to party or something. He'll chase us off and that'll be the end of it."

"*If* he catches us, which he won't," Annie

added emphatically. "What do you have to lose by letting us try, Mr. Riverwind?"

"Nothing." The old man smiled.

"There's one condition, though," Annie added. "Your people have to stay away from the lake until midnight."

"Agreed, but I'd feel better if we could do something to help," Mr. Riverwind said.

"You can." Annie smiled back. "Danielle Atron's trespassing warning doesn't apply to the ridge above the lake because it's on the reservation, right?"

"That's right." Nathan looked up with renewed interest.

"Can you get the whole tribe to gather on the ridge at midnight and stay hidden until the plant truck arrives?" Annie asked.

"Yes," Mr. Riverwind said.

He did not ask why, and Alex was touched by his unquestioning acceptance. Most of the time, adults didn't give kids much credit. The old man's trust made her take her responsibility much more seriously.

Alex watched Nathan and his grandfather leave. They were smiling as they said their goodbyes and seemed to be more hopeful than when they'd arrived.

For perhaps the first time, Alex fully realized that along with her powers came some pretty big responsibilities. And it made her feel a little shaky. What if she failed?

CHAPTER 11

Alex, Annie, and Ray arrived at the lake late that afternoon. With Mr. Riverwind's permission, Annie parked the car around a bend on the reservation branch of the dirt road. Lugging a picnic cooler and other supplies, they all glanced back at the car when they reached the fork.

"Can't see it." Ray smiled and adjusted his grip on the cooler handle.

Annie nodded, but continued to frown. "Now we just have to hope Dave doesn't take a wrong turn on his way in here."

"Even if he does, Vince'll think the car belongs to someone on the reservation," Alex said. Carrying blankets, towels, and Ray's black bag, she led the way up the incline toward the lake. "I just wish we had gotten an earlier start."

"If you ask me, it's a good thing we decided to finish stacking the packed boxes in the garage," said Annie, who was holding on to the other cooler handle. She struggled to keep up with Ray's long strides.

"I'll say. We would have missed Mom and Dad's call," Alex said.

"She was sure excited about making it to the semifinal round this afternoon." Annie grunted as they neared the top of the rise.

"Are you sure they won't call back tonight?" Ray asked.

"I'm not positive, but I doubt it." Breathing heavily, Annie stopped and motioned for Ray to set down the cooler. "They think we're going to a double feature that doesn't end until midnight, and Dad wants Mom in bed and asleep by ten."

Getting the phone call from their parents had made their plan go so much easier, Alex thought. But she was starting to get a little nervous about her uncanny good luck. Either fate was working with them to help the tribe and save the lake— or the luck was going to run out any minute. Getting caught by her sister sneaking back home after a surveillance mission with Ray had been to her advantage, since Annie had decided to be on her side. And meeting Nathan and his grandfather had also helped their cause. But Alex feared that her lucky streak couldn't possibly last.

"What if Mom doesn't make the finals tomorrow?" Alex said. She couldn't help being worried. Her mom might be so disappointed about losing the tennis tournament, she'd want to come home tonight. It was only a two-hour drive.

"Dad said they're staying to watch, no matter what." Breathing in deeply several times, Annie picked up the cooler again. "Good sportsmanship and all that."

"Uh-huh." Alex kicked stones as she trudged down the hill to the beach. "Do you think Dad'll be really upset if we don't get the garage done? What if he decides to finish it himself and finds the GC-161 stuff?"

Annie sighed and shook her head. "I'll handle that problem when and if it happens, so stop worrying, Alex. We're here, and we've got an important job to do. That's all we should be thinking about right now."

"She's right, Alex," Ray said solemnly. "I've hardly given my newspaper story a thought. This is even more important than my byline. We've got to concentrate on what we're doing—especially you. Without you, there is no Operation Coyote."

Alex was very aware of that. Pausing by the water's edge, she closed her eyes and listened to the gentle lapping of the lake around her boots.

Success depended solely on her and her amazing powers. In a way, it was funny and fitting that the bizarre effects of the plant's illegal compound, GC-161, would be used to fight the tribe's environmental battle. After two years of eluding Vince and learning to cope with the genetic changes, Alex welcomed the opportunity to strike back for a just cause. Deliberately using her powers against Danielle Atron to end Paradise Valley Chemical's dangerous dumping of toxic waste would be a personal triumph. If Alex succeeded.

Annie stepped up beside her and scanned the shoreline. "Why would anyone want to destroy such a beautiful place?"

Alex opened her eyes and surveyed the mountain lake in silent agreement. She hadn't seen it in the daytime before. Birds sang in tall evergreen pines, and small animals rustled through the brush in search of last-minute provisions for the cold months ahead. The orange and red leaves on hardwood branches danced in a light breeze, and sunlight sparkled off the lake under a clear blue sky. It was warmer than usual for an October day, like summer had returned for a quick farewell before passing the seasonal torch on to winter.

Alex sighed wistfully. It was worth any risk to save the lake and the land around it. Nicole—champion of many worthy causes—would be proud of her. But Nicole would never know. No one would know except Annie and Ray—and possibly some fish and frogs, Alex thought with a smile—but that was as it should be. Stopping the contamination was all that mattered.

"So where do we start?" Ray skipped a flat stone across the water and gave himself a fisted salute when it bounced three times before sinking.

"First I've got to find all those barrels." Alex frowned as she gazed toward the middle of the lake. It would be like trying to find pennies in a big sandbox. Not impossible, but not exactly a snap, either.

"You go with Alex in the boat, Ray," Annie said. "I'll set up camp over there." She pointed to a mound of rocks farther down the shore. "It's secluded, but close enough to the beach so Alex can get in and out without too much trouble later."

After they had helped carry everything to Annie's site, Alex stripped down to the bathing suit she was wearing under her clothes. Although the air was warm, the deep lake water would be cold. She'd have to morph repeatedly without getting out of the water, and the weight of wet clothes would tire her more quickly. She only hoped that cold and exhaustion didn't get the best of her before she finished the initial phase of their plan.

Tossing Ray a life preserver, Alex slipped into hers and sat in the bow as he untied the line, pushed the boat into the water, and jumped in. As he rowed toward the middle of the lake, the breeze picked up and Alex shivered. The air was cooling as the sun dipped lower in the sky. They had only a couple hours of daylight left to locate the sunken barrels. If she didn't find them before dark, Operation Coyote would be over before it started.

"About here, don't you think?" Ray shifted the oars.

"We'll know soon enough." With a curt wave, Alex liquefied and slid out of the boat. The warming that flooded through her during the transformation process chilled suddenly. Her liquid-cells went rigid with the shock.

Heavier than water and stiff with cold, Alex sank like a rock.

CHAPTER 12

Above her, Alex saw the sunlight on the surface of the water fade as she sank deeper and deeper. The life preserver was useless because it had become part of her morphed-self, just like her bathing suit. Fighting a sudden panic, she forced herself to relax. It was impossible to drown in her morphed state, but she could only stay morphed for five minutes. She couldn't be stuck on the bottom when her cells insisted on changing back to normal again. That would be disastrous!

Forming into a flattened ribbon, Alex propelled herself downward with a rippling, fishtail motion. Her movements were more sluggish than usual because of the cold water temperature, but she was moving.

The eerie, absolute silence that reigned in the deep water enhanced her sense of isolation. She was alone except for a school of small fish that abruptly changed direction and fled when she passed. Skimming the murky bottom, Alex felt like an alien exploring a strange and distant world. The sensation was both exciting and frightening.

It was difficult to see in the twilight of filtered sunshine that reached the lake floor. Tangles of weeds and pieces of water-logged wood littered the bottom, which was covered with muck. Alex figured the bright yellow barrels would be visible within a range of ten feet or so—unless the weighted containers had settled too deep in the squishy mire.

Recently, Alex had been trying to make distinct formations with her liquid body, but she wasn't very good at it yet. Concentrating, she managed to create a long, thin protrusion and stick it in the muck. A large, dark fish darted out from behind a rock to investigate. Alex tensed as it gently nibbled her probing "arm." Then, deciding that the strange, silvery invader was not a new food source, it lazily swam away. Watching the fish had a profound effect on Alex. It didn't have a clue that its safe and secure underwater home was being threatened with destruction. Shaking the disturbing thought from her mind, she turned her attention back to the muck.

She found that the mud was only a few inches deep, not enough to bury the barrels. With that worry eliminated, Alex swam an ever-widening circular pattern and kept a lookout for anything yellow in the murky brown depths.

When she surfaced after a fruitless search and materialized as her normal self, Ray exhaled anxiously.

"What's the matter?" she asked. The re-materialized life preserver was working now, and Alex bobbed in the water next to the boat. Looking toward shore, she wondered if Vince had arrived early, but the beach was empty.

"I was afraid something happened to you." Ray looked at his watch. "You were down there for over seven minutes."

"Seven minutes? Wow!" Alex said. She had materialized by choice just now, not because the morphing state had exceeded its built-in time limit. "Make a mental note for Annie, Ray. Apparently I can stay morphed longer in cold temperatures."

Alex shook her head in wonder. Instead of being a problem, the cold water was going to make her job a lot easier. The luck had not deserted her—yet.

Alex stayed in the water and clung to the boat as Ray rowed from spot to spot. She finally found the yellow barrels strewn along the mucky bottom on her fourth dive.

"How many are down there?" Ray asked.

"Six, just like Nathan thought. I hope that's all of them, because we don't have time to cover the whole lake."

Shivering and tired, Alex wished she could rest, but time was running out. She looked toward the western horizon. The sun would disappear behind the mountain within minutes, and she wasn't finished yet. The weights were secured to the barrels by lengths of chain looped through the handles and tied. Alex still had to loosen the knots.

Drawing on her last bit of reserved energy, Alex morphed and dove again. The first barrel was lying on its side with the chained handle up. Elongating, Alex flowed through the loop in the chain, then expanded her liquid form to force the knot apart. Fortunately, the barrels had not been submerged long enough to rust the metal, so the chain was easy to slide. Leaving the untied length of chain looped through the handle to keep the barrel weighted, Alex surfaced. The sky grayed in the few minutes she took to catch her breath. She'd have to untie the rest of the knots in the dark.

Exhausted and freezing in the evening air, Alex morphed on sheer will power that was reinforced by Ray's constant encouragement. Forced to surface after she had taken care of each barrel, she found she needed longer and longer rest periods between transformations. She stubbornly tackled the task in spite of a growing weakness in every cell—liquid and solid. Another two hours passed before she finally dragged herself back into the boat and collapsed.

"What time is it?" Alex asked, gasping.

"Almost eight."

Nodding, Alex closed her eyes. Lulled by the rocking of the boat on the water, she hovered between being awake and asleep as Ray wrapped her in dry blankets. Anxious about getting caught out on the lake if Vince showed up ahead of schedule, she fought her body's desperate demand for sleep and forced her eyes open. A half-moon was just rising, and she inhaled softly when she saw a shadowy figure standing on the beach. It was Annie.

"Did everything go okay?" Annie asked as she waded into the water to help Ray pull the boat up to the anchor log.

"Yeah, it just took longer than we expected." Ray glanced at Alex with a worried frown. "I'm not sure Alex is okay, though."

Leaving Ray to secure the bow line to the log, Annie rushed to the side of the boat. "What's the matter?"

"Nothing, just tired. I could sleep for a week." Pulling herself to her feet, Alex stumbled out of the boat.

Annie grabbed her arm to steady her. "You don't have a week, I'm afraid to say. You've only got four hours, and if we don't get you into dry clothes right away, you'll have pneumonia before the plant truck gets here."

"Can't have that," Alex mumbled, then giggled softly. "I just fall apart when I sneeze." She had caught a cold from Ray once, which had made her morph into tiny droplets every time she sneezed. Somehow she had to find the strength to hang on until Operation Coyote was completed.

While Ray used a branch to erase the boat trail and their footprints off the sandy shore, Annie draped an arm around Alex's shoulders and guided her to their concealed campsite. With Annie's help, Alex slipped back into her clothes. Being warm and dry made it impossible to resist the overwhelming weariness any longer. She curled up in dry blankets and immediately fell into an oblivion of exhaustion.

The next thing Alex knew, Annie was shaking her awake. "Come on, Alex. It's after midnight."

Alex sat up with a start and blinked as her eyes adjusted to the dim moonlight. Annie and Ray were sitting in the dark, because a fire or flashlight would give their presence and position away to Vince. "Are they here?"

"Not yet," Ray said.

"What about Nathan and the others?" Alex asked.

"We hope they're hidden up on the ridge," Annie said.

Alex fell back on the blankets. "Wake me up when Vince and Dave get here."

"Alex," Annie said sharply, "you've got to eat something to build up your strength or the trickster coyote won't be able to play any pranks."

"Okay." Sighing, Alex took the sandwich Annie handed her and stared at it. She was famished, but at the moment chewing seemed like too much work.

Ray was sitting with his back to a large rock a few feet away. He took a bite of his sandwich, chewed, swallowed, then frowned. "Pass me a can of soda, please."

Alex automatically reached out with her thoughts and grabbed an orange pop out of the open cooler. It seemed terribly heavy as she telekinetically guided it toward Ray.

"Alex, must you?" Annie asked.

Annie's words cut through Alex's concentration. Her thoughts and the can wobbled. The telekinetic connection broke, and the can landed on the ground with a thud.

"Halfway's better than nothing, I guess." Ray leaned over to pick up the soda can.

"I didn't do that on purpose." Alarmed, Alex tried to telekinetically yank the can from Ray's hand. She couldn't.

"Meaning?" Annie peered at her through the dark.

Numb, Alex stared back. "Meaning I'm so tired I couldn't hold onto it."

Annie's eyes widened.

Ray looked confused. "If you're too tired to move a can of soda, how are you going to pull six heavy barrels of chemicals off the bottom of the lake?"

"I don't know." Shaking her head in despair, Alex gazed out over the moonlit water. Vince was smart, confident, and tough. It would take something spectacular and totally inexplicable to scare him into believing that the trickster coyote was a powerful force and not just a Native American fairy tale. Or a couple of kids fooling around.

The sound of an engine rumbled through the forest quiet.

Alex crept up beside Annie and Ray as they cautiously looked over the top of the large rock. The beam of headlights grew brighter as the plant truck crawled to the crest of the rise.

"Watch it, Dave!" Vince's barking voice rang out clearly through the open cab window as the truck lurched over a deep rut. "You're supposed to miss the potholes, not hit them!"

"Sorry, Vince."

Alex swallowed hard. She *had* to move the barrels or the plan would fail and the lake would be lost. So many people were depending on her—and her alone. She wouldn't get a second chance.

CHAPTER 13

Dave, the PVC driver, parked the truck close to the water's edge with the back end facing the lake. He stepped out of the cab and slammed the door, then stretched and breathed in the crisp mountain air. He was wearing a blue uniform that said Paradise Valley Chemical on the back.

"We're not here to get closer to nature, Dave." Vince rounded the front of the truck. Wearing jeans, a turtleneck and black parka, he scanned the forest with a high-powered flashlight.

Alex, Ray, and Annie ducked.

"I know, Vince. We're here to dump those barrels because nobody else would do the job."

"They all might be out of jobs completely after

I catch Mr. Riverwind and his grandson messing around on plant property." Vince hitched up his jeans and stared into the dark woods. "When I prove that the old man and his people scared them off with a bunch of Halloween tricks, they'll all feel like the sniveling cowards they are."

Dave shrugged. "What if Mr. Riverwind didn't do it?"

Vince shook his head in disgust. "Only a fool would believe in a mythical coyote that prowls the woods bent on revenge. Get started now, Dave. I don't want to be out here all night."

"What are you gonna do?"

"I'm gonna scout the area." Vince walked toward the trees in front of the truck, away from the campsite.

Alex, Annie, and Ray huddled behind the large rock.

"What if he finds us?" Ray hissed softly.

"We'd better make sure that he doesn't." Annie handed Alex her sandwich. "Finish this. It'll help you get your strength back." Then she quietly began picking up the remains of their midnight snack and putting it in the cooler. Ray helped.

Chewing absently, Alex watched Dave as he opened the cargo doors and climbed inside.

Grunting and huffing, he pushed a barrel to the edge of the loading ramp. The sight of the yellow container triggered dark images in her mind. She saw big fish floating dead in the water and trees withering along the shore, victims of the chemical plant's poison time bombs. The gruesome mental pictures ignited a determined fury inside her.

"Vince!" Dave yelled. "I can't get these in the boat without some help! They're too heavy!"

Annie, Alex, and Ray froze as brush and tree branches rattled a short distance away. Vince stomped out of the forest and passed a few feet in front of the large rock they were hiding behind. Turning off the flashlight, he clipped it to his belt and strolled back to Dave.

Alex exhaled quietly. She hadn't even been aware of holding her breath. Luck was still on her side, and she could only hope it would last long enough. Swallowing the last bite of her sandwich, Alex carefully moved over to the pile of blankets. She slipped out of her jacket and put on a life preserver.

"What are you doing?" Annie whispered.

"Going out on the lake." Alex untied her boots and pulled them off. Her telekinetic powers had gotten stronger as she had gotten older. The weakness she had experienced with the soda can might be only temporary, but she couldn't take the chance. "I've got to get closer to those barrels to lift them."

"You can't! You'll freeze out there at night!" Annie grabbed her arm.

"I have to." Alex held Annie's worried gaze a long moment, then morphed and slid out of her sister's grasp. As she slithered away, she heard Annie and Ray whispering.

"Just sit tight, Ray, and be quiet."

"Right, except I gotta howl when Alex—"

"No! Vince will just think somebody from the tribe is doing it, and the noise will give away our position."

"But—"

"No howling." Annie meant it.

Materializing behind a large log, Alex chanced a peek to check Vince and Dave's progress. Vince was in the boat with the barrel, and Dave was struggling to launch it into the lake. Bracing herself, Alex morphed again and glided silently into the brutally cold water.

Prepared for the shock this time, Alex recovered quickly. She elongated and skimmed the surface with a snakelike motion. Pacing the boat, she quickly realized that Dave didn't know where the other men had pushed their barrels overboard. He stopped rowing about fifty feet from the original dump site.

One thing at a time, Alex thought as she materialized a short distance astern of the boat. Her teeth started to chatter as she bobbed in the chilling water, but the rattling of the weight chain against the metal container covered the soft clicking sound. Concentrating her diminished energies, Alex threw up an electromagnetic force field as Vince and Dave lifted the barrel and tried to roll it overboard.

Vince and Dave pushed.

The barrel refused to fall.

"Are you stepping on the chain or what?" Vince asked.

Dave looked down. "Nope."

"Then why can't we shove it off the boat?" Vince barked in frustration.

"Beats me, Vince." Taking his hands off the barrel, Dave stared at it and scratched his head. "Kinda weird, huh?"

Moving the force field, Alex pushed the barrel back into the boat. Startled, Dave stumbled back and almost fell out. Vince grabbed his shirt and they both sat down with a loud thump.

Morphing instantly, Alex zipped through the water to the other site and dove to pinpoint the position of the submerged barrels. She surfaced and materialized just as Vince and Dave began lifting their barrel again. With no time to waste, she visualized the barrels lying on the bottom. When she felt her thoughts "touch" cold, hard metal, she telekinetically slipped the loose chain through the handle. That was easy enough, but when she tried to move the barrel, it wouldn't budge.

Desperation sent waves of energy coursing through her. Reaching out again, she grabbed the barrel with her mind and yanked it to the surface. She had heard stories about little old ladies who mysteriously developed the strength to lift cars in an emergency. The same thing was happening to her.

Supercharged with adrenaline and urgency, Alex sent the barrel skating across the top of the water toward the rowboat.

Dave dropped his end of the barrel and pointed. "What's that?"

Vince's head snapped around. "What's wha—"

His mouth fell open as the yellow torpedo zeroed in on its target.

Just before the barrel plowed into the boat, Alex turned it sharply and sent it skimming toward shore. When it rolled onto the beach, she immediately grabbed a second barrel off the bottom.

Paralyzed in surprise and disbelief, Vince and Dave watched as the second barrel rocketed across the water, onto the beach, and clanged into the first one.

Alex heard the whisper of a chant begin as she brought another barrel up and sent it bouncing over the surface of the lake. The chant grew steadily louder and increased in tempo as the third container joined its beached companions by the truck. Alex glanced upward to see everyone from Nathan's tribe lining up along the ridge. Bathed in dim moonlight, they looked like shadowy ghosts from a long-ago past. They were calling the trickster coyote, but the sight and sound fueled the energies driving her.

The specter on the ridge also convinced Vince that he should get out of there—fast. But he could only go as fast as Dave could row. With glee, Alex steered the fourth barrel so it paced the rowboat for a moment.

"Put some muscle into it, Dave!" Vince shouted fiercely.

Dave frantically dipped and pulled the oars, then relaxed when the barrel suddenly shot toward the beach. "That is so cool!" he said.

"Out of my way!" Vince pushed Dave aside and took over, rowing at a furious rate. All six barrels were piled on the beach when Vince and Dave finally reached shore.

Morphing, Alex raced across the water. She slithered behind the log and materialized as the security man and driver leaped out of the boat and ran for the cab.

"What about the barrels?" Dave asked.

"Leave 'em!"

I don't think so, Vince. Alex telekinetically slammed the cab doors closed and locked them so that the two men couldn't get in the truck and drive off.

Vince jumped, flattening his back against the side of the truck, and swept the woods with a wide-eyed gaze.

Dave pulled on his door handle several times. "It's locked. How are we supposed to get out of here? The keys are still in the ignition."

Before Vince could answer, Alex lifted the barrel out of the boat. With a final burst of energy, she heaved it through the cargo doors into the rear of the truck.

The tribe's chanting stopped suddenly.

Vince and Dave rushed to the back of the truck to look.

"Maybe the coyote will let us go if we take the barrels with us," Dave suggested.

Exhausted and shivering uncontrollably in her wet clothes, Alex took a deep breath. She didn't think she had enough strength left to lift a pencil, but she had to move one of the barrels one more time. Beads of sweat broke out on her forehead as she concentrated and slowly rolled a yellow container up the beach toward the truck.

Dave's comment pierced Vince's abnormal state of confusion and fear. "Don't be ridiculous, Dave. There is no coyote—"

A mournful howl rose from high on the mountain and echoed across the lake.

Moving in perfect sync, Vince and Dave looked toward the mountain, down at the barrel as it rolled to a stop between them, then at each other.

"Maybe Ms. Atron should take the hint, Vince, and find some other way to get rid of this stuff."

"Exactly what I was thinking." Vince and Dave

lifted the barrel and set it inside the truck. As they moved to pick up another one, Vince grabbed Dave's arm. "But none of this ever happened."

"Yes, it did." Dave blinked. "The barrels popped out of the lake—"

Vince's eyes narrowed and his voice filled with menace. *"This—did—not—happen!* And if you ever say it did—you're fired!"

Alex smiled. Vince's reputation as a tough security man would be ruined if anyone knew he had been frightened and run off by a mythical coyote's pranks.

"You can't fire me, Vince," Dave said as they loaded another barrel. "I'm the only guy who can identify the GC-161 kid, remember?"

"How can I forget?" Vince kicked the fourth barrel in frustrated anger before he picked it up.

Dave frowned thoughtfully as they shoved it into the truck. "How are you going to convince Ms. Atron to spend money on waste disposal if this didn't happen?"

"Easy. PVC is concerned about the environment. That's good for the company's public image." Vince paused to catch his breath. "If she sells this land to the tribe, she can use the money to build a safe disposal system."

"Works for me." When the remaining barrels were inside, Dave closed and latched the cargo doors.

Works for me, too, Alex thought as she stretched out on the ground. She dozed off to the sound of the truck driving away, never to return.

And a distant coyote howl.

CHAPTER 14

Alex drifted in a dreamy doze, exhausted but still too excited to surrender to deep sleep. She heard Ray whisper as he hovered over her, "Is she okay?"

"I sure hope so." Annie brushed Alex's wet hair off her face. "Why don't you take our stuff to the road while I help her into some dry clothes." As Ray hurried away, Annie gently touched Alex's shoulder.

Alex sat up, feeling strangely refreshed after her short nap. "We did it, Annie."

"*You* did it," Annie replied, handing Alex her clothes. Annie smiled as she held up a blanket to shield her sister from the cold. "And you were terrific! This is one time I'm glad you used your powers in public. And Vince won't ever be the same! But I'm a little worried about what he's going to tell Danielle Atron.''

"He's going to tell her to sell the land and use the money to build a safe disposal plant." Shrugging out of her wet shirt, Alex pulled the dry one over her head. "He told Dave he'd fire him if he said *anything* about what happened here tonight."

"Lucky for us."

Alex only nodded as she finished changing and followed Annie across the beach to the road. Ray was sitting on the cooler. "How are you feeling, Alex?" he asked.

"Great." And that was the truth, Alex realized as she stuffed her wet clothes in a plastic garbage bag with the soggy blankets. Picking up the bag, she fell into step with Annie and Ray as they started up the incline. Now that she was warm and dry, the crisp mountain air felt invigorating. More important, Operation Coyote had been one hundred percent successful.

"I owe you both a big thanks," Alex said. "I couldn't have pulled this off without your help."

Ray shrugged. "We didn't do much."

"Yes, you did!" Alex insisted. "We couldn't

have gotten here if Annie hadn't agreed to drive. And we wouldn't even have known about the danger to the lake if you hadn't been so determined to write a story for the *Paradise Valley Press*."

"You've got one whopper of a scoop for your editor, Ray," Annie said. "I'd say your career as an investigative reporter is off to a good start."

"Yeah. It's everything I wanted my first story to be, and Mr. Hardwick's gonna love it, but it'll be my last story."

"Why?" the girls asked in mutual surprise.

"For one thing, I'll never be able to top it." Ray grinned. "And for another, I can't write about the best part."

"The trickster coyote?" Annie asked.

"You got it." Ray shifted his grip on the cooler as they turned onto the reservation branch of the dirt track.

"That howl of yours put Vince over the edge, Ray. It's a good thing you didn't keep quiet like Annie wanted," Alex said.

Ray stared at her. "I didn't howl. We thought you did."

"Not me." Alex frowned. "One of Nathan's friends, maybe?"

No one answered. Their attention was drawn to a glow of flickering firelight. As they rounded the curve where the car was parked, they stopped dead in their tracks. Nathan's entire tribe was standing in the road. Men, women, and children stared at them with dark eyes that glinted in the light of several torches.

Clutching the plastic bag closer, Alex glanced at Annie, then back at the crowd as Nathan's grandfather stepped forward. He was wearing jeans, a plaid shirt, and boots. His expression was stern, and his piercing gaze was fastened on her. Alex tensed, wondering if she had broken some ancient taboo or something.

Then suddenly, Mr. Riverwind smiled and gave her a thumbs-up. Everyone broke into resounding applause and cheers. Nathan ran forward and took the plastic bag from her hands. Two other boys relieved Annie and Ray of the cooler and the black bag. Then the three of them were swept along with the crowd into the forest.

Nathan grinned broadly. "Hope you guys aren't too worn out to party. This celebration is in your honor."

Awed, Alex watched as men with torches lit a bonfire set up in the middle of a large clearing.

Picnic tables were piled high with food and sodas. Two women and three men picked up instruments and launched into a lively, traditional native song. Children whooped around the fire and couples started to dance.

"This is for us?" Alex was so overwhelmed, her eyes misted.

"It's not much of a thank-you for what you did for us—" Nathan began.

"Are you kidding? It's great!" Alex laughed.

"Although," Nathan continued, "no one is exactly sure *what* you did."

"Does it really matter?" Annie asked.

"No. It worked, and that's all that counts," Nathan said in agreement.

"Just out of curiosity . . ." Ray leaned closer to Nathan and lowered his voice. "Did someone on the ridge howl?"

Nathan laughed aloud. "You're joking, right?"

"Right." With a perplexed glance at Alex, Ray made a beeline for the food.

Annie frowned and stared deeply into the fire, then was distracted when a young man asked her to dance. She hesitated, shrugged an "okay," and was instantly whirled away.

Nathan shifted his weight self-consciously. "All

kidding aside, I don't know how you guys rigged that stunt with the barrels, but it was spectacular. Those guys won't be coming back, and Danielle Atron is history."

"Not quite."

A scowl darkened Nathan's face. "What do you mean?"

Alex smiled mischievously. "I wouldn't be surprised if she takes you up on your offer to buy the lake."

"Really?" Nathan jumped with excitement, then shook his head with amazement. "If I didn't know better, I'd think the trickster coyote had appeared to avenge us for real." A woman called his name and waved him over. "My mom. I'll be right back."

"Okay."

Mr. Riverwind spoke softly from behind Alex. "There are many here tonight who no longer doubt. Someday Nathan, too, will realize that the trickster coyote *did* come. A very young, pretty, and unusual trickster coyote."

Alex looked back at him with a startled gasp. *He knows!*

The old man raised an eyebrow and his wise,

knowing eyes sparkled as he continued. "You had some help from the spirit coyote."

Alex blinked. "The spirit coyote?"

"Think about it." The old man looked toward the high mountain for a long moment, then winked as he walked away.

Alex noticed how people watched with respect as he passed. True to his beliefs and the ancient traditions, Mr. Riverwind had summoned the trickster coyote to help them, and his call had been answered.

Standing alone on the edge of the woods, Alex shivered. She wasn't cold. She was thrilled by the truth in the old shaman's words. Strange and inexplicable things *did* happen. She was certain he would never tell anyone about her powers, and she was glad they had helped him regain the tribe's faith and confidence in his wisdom.

But she hadn't done it alone.

The incredible good luck she had met at every turn might have been coincidence, but she didn't really think so.

Maybe it was a romantic notion, but Alex was sure she had been protected and helped by the *real* trickster coyote.

*   *   *

133

Alex woke up with a start and looked at the clock beside her bed. The digital readout said 3:12.

Throwing off the covers, she jumped out of bed. She was still wearing the clothes she had on last night. The last thing she remembered was getting into the car to come home at four o'clock that morning. She had fallen asleep the instant she stretched out on the back seat. And she had slept until three o'clock in the afternoon even though the garage was still a wreck!

Taking a few minutes to brush her teeth, comb her tangled hair, and splash cold water on her face, Alex dashed out of the bathroom. As she started down the stairs, she heard the answering machine beeping in her parents' bedroom and went in to retrieve the messages. There was only one—from her excited mother.

"... thrilled to know that Mrs. Lincoln and I won the women's doubles. The award banquet starts at five, so we probably won't make it home until late. Don't wait up. Love you."

Pleased by her mother's victory and glad to have a few more hours to work on the garage, Alex raced downstairs.

She called, "Annie!" Finding the living room deserted, Alex wandered into the kitchen. Although she knew everything about the lake, the yellow barrels, Vince and Dave, the trickster coyote, and the tribe's wonderful party had really happened, it all seemed like a bizarre dream in the light of day.

But it was no dream. The cooler was sitting on the kitchen floor, empty and drying out. And the Sunday edition of the *Paradise Valley Press* was on the counter. The headline was printed in huge black letters.

PVC ALMOST POISONS LAKE
by Jeremy Hardwick and Ray Alvarado

Alex quickly scanned the short article. There was no mention of her or the trickster coyote, but the story accurately reported that the plant had been dumping chemical waste in the remote lake, and that the neighboring Native American tribe was pressuring Danielle Atron to utilize a safer method of disposal. If nothing else, the article would force the CEO to take Vince's advice.

The story had been written days ago, and Ray had probably gotten Mr. Hardwick out of bed to tell him to print it in the Sunday edition. A longer, in-depth story was promised for a later edition.

Then Alex heard voices in the garage.

She threw open the door, expecting to find Annie and Ray. She did not expect to see Annie and Ray plus Nathan and four other kids from the tribe.

Or a garage that was in near-perfect order.

Stunned, Alex stood in the open doorway and stared. Everything was neatly stacked, shelved, or hanging in precise rows on pegboard hooks. Nathan was sweeping a large, cleared area of the floor. His friends carried trash bags out the front door. Ray was folding clean blankets while Annie transferred a load of washed clothes into the drier.

"Hey, sleepyhead. It's about time you got up." Annie looked up with a scowl, then smiled.

Nathan stopped sweeping and leaned on the broom handle. "Surprise!"

"What are you doing here, Nathan?" Alex asked as she stepped into the garage.

"Returning a favor. When Annie told us about your garage problem, my friends and I decided to pitch in and help. What do you think?"

"This is amazing."

Nathan looked around with a satisfied nod. "Not nearly as amazing as your impersonation of the trickster coyote, but we've got a few tricks of our own."

"Not quite as many tricks as Alex, though." Ray put the stack of blankets on the drier, then howled.

Everyone laughed.

Alex just smiled. Nathan and his friends wouldn't believe the truth any more than they'd believe an ordinary teen-age girl had fantastic powers. But she knew.

In the deep forest high on a mountain, the trickster coyote was having the last laugh.

About the Author

Diana G. Gallagher lives in Kansas with her husband, Marty Burke, two dogs, three cats, and a cranky parrot. When she's not writing, she likes to read and take long walks with the dogs.

A Hugo Award-winning illustrator, she is best known for her series *Woof: The House Dragon.* Her songs about humanity's future are sung throughout the world and have been recorded in cassette form: "Cosmic Concepts More Complete," Star*Song," and "Fire Dream." Diana and Marty, an Irish folksinger, perform traditional and original music at science-fiction conventions.

Her first adult novel, *The Alien Dark*, appeared in 1990. She is also the author of a *Star Trek: Deep Space Nine®* novel for young readers, *Arcade*, and five other books in *The Secret World of Alex Mack* series, all available from Minstrel Books.

She is currently working on another *Star Trek* novel and a new *Alex Mack* story.